"NBC's new animated *Star Trek* is . . . fascinating fare, written, produced and executed with all the imaginative skill, the intellectual flare and the literary level that made Gene Roddenberry's famous old science-fiction epic the most avidly followed program in TV history . . ."

—Cecil Smith
The Los Angeles Times

STAR TREK

The show that would not die . . .

Back in 1966 Gene Roddenberry convinced NBC-TV to give sophisticated science fiction a try, and *Star Trek* was launched. Getting the show on the air was a triumph in itself; keeping it on the air was something else again. Toward the end of the second season there were rumors of impending cancellation.

Viewers passionately devoted to the series deluged the network with letters of protest. Loyal fans picketed NBC's offices both in California and New York. The Save Star Trek Campaign—one of the most phenomenal expressions of viewer interest in the history of tv—worked.

So *Star Trek* was back on the air for a third season. Alas, however, many factors combined to lower the program's ratings, giving the network the ammunition it needed to cancel the series.

But still the fans wanted more . . .

Books about *Star Trek* were published, each one selling hundreds of thousands of copies to the faithful. *Star Trek* conventions all over the country attracted thousands of fans.

And now we have the exciting animated *Star Trek*. All the original actors (at least their voices) are back aboard the starship *Enterprise,* assuring success.

Ballantine proudly launches the STAR TREK LOG series, publishing all the exciting new stories in paperback for the first time.

STAR TREK LIVES!

STAR TREK
LOG TWO

Alan Dean Foster

**Based on the Popular Animated Series Created by
GENE RODDENBERRY**

A Del Rey Book

BALLANTINE BOOKS • NEW YORK

A Del Rey Book
Published by Ballantine Books

Library of Congress Catalog Card Number: 74-8477

ISBN 0-345-28265-5

Manufactured in the United States of America

First Edition: September 1974
Eleventh Printing: December 1979

Cover art by Stanislaw Fernandes

For Mom & Dad,

Without whose sincere cooperation,
This author wouldn't have been possible

CONTENTS

STAR TREK LOG TWO

Log of the Starship *Enterprise*

Stardates 5402.7–5503.1 Inclusive

James T. Kirk, Capt., USSC, FS, ret.

Commanding

transcribed by
Alan Dean Foster

At the Galactic Historical Archives
on S. Monicus I
stardated 6110.5

For the Curator: JLR

PART I

THE SURVIVOR

(Adapted from a script by James Schmerer)

1

Space is not silent.

If one has the ears—the appropriate methods to listen with—the seeming emptiness and black desolation is transformed into a raucous chorus of bleeps, pops, whistles, and hums. The steady modulated whines of patient quasars, the discordant sizzle of black holes, and the stentorian drone of unseen pulsars—all contribute their voices to a heavenly choir of awesome complexity and rhythm.

From white dwarf to red giant, every sun exhibits its own distinctive, individual sizzle-plop in the same way that animals give off special odors, or flowers display color.

At this particular moment, in this typically insignificant corner of the universe, an exceptionally unusual sound was being generated. It came from a minute, irregularly shaped and rapidly moving object of considerably less than solar mass. And yet the sounds it was producing were at once less powerful and more distinctive than those given off by any sun, or pulsar, or radio nebula.

Anyone passing near this object would have needed very, very sensitive instruments indeed to pick up the sound at all. But if one *had* the proper detection equipment and an enormous quantity of amplification at immediate disposal, one might just be able to hear:

"Deck the halls with boughs of holly, fa-lalala-lala-lalala . . . 'Tis the season to be jolly, fa. . . !"

But by then, of course, the *Enterprise* would have shot far out of detector range.

Once a year the tree was carefully unwrapped and lifted from its special cold-storage compartment in the bottom of

3

the starship's cold-storage room. Then, amid much gaiety and boozing, it was set up in the main crew lounge and decorated with everything from genuine gingerbread cookies to holographic angels.

It was a real evergreen, too—as fine and upstanding a tannenbaum as any celebrant could wish for. No one minded that it had sprung from the soil of a world unknown to Man when words were first spoken on his moon.

A group of engineers and technicians had organized an unprofessional but enthusiastic barbershop quartet near the base of the glowing tree. They were caroling away lustily to the accompaniment of a small electric piano.

Lt. Uhura leaned against the fake fireplace set up nearby. She was talking to a tall young ensign from quartermaster section. Every so often she'd emphasize some point or other by jabbing him in the chest with a finger—one of those not wrapped around a glass.

For his part, the ensign was still unsure about how to react. On the one hand, the sudden unexpected situation involving the most desirable lieutenant on the ship was developing promisingly. On the other, he couldn't forget that she was his superior officer. Given the current lack of equilibrium the senior lieutenant was displaying, he'd have to be careful things didn't turn awkward.

"Lischen . . . listen, Ensign Burns . . . I tell you there's nothing like working in communications! Communication is the most important, most necessariest section on this ship. Why, without communication we . . . we couldn't talk to each other!" She seemed overwhelmed at this sudden insight.

"I ask you . . . where'd the *Enterprise* be without communications? Where!"

"I couldn't agree with you more, Lieutenant," agreed Burns, cautiously slipping an agreeing arm around her shoulders. "Of course, we should bear in mind that there are all kinds of communication . . . here, let me get you a refill. I have some interesting theories of my own which I'm sure would benefit greatly from the comments and suggestions of a senior officer like yourself.

"If you could spare a minute . . . I've drawn up some interesting schematics that . . ."

On the far side of the lounge, Engineer Scott had corralled Spock at an unoccupied table. The surface between them was swamped with seemingly numberless sheets of paper filled with hurriedly roughed-out engineering diagrams.

"Now you see here, Spock," Scott was saying intensely, tracing a rather wobbly line on one sheet with his drafting pen, "this is—" He paused and stared disapprovingly at the *Enterprise*'s first officer.

"Och, smile, Spock, why don't you? 'Tis the season to be jolly, fa-lalala . . ."

Spock's reaction was similar to the one he'd already used several times that day, in response to the sudden explosion of illogical activity. To him this "season" seemed a cyclical madness that, fortunately, had to be borne only once a year.

But, by Vulcan's long deserts, it was hard on him.

"I am sorry, Mr. Scott. First of all, I do not 'fa-lala,' as you well know. Also, even if this were my holiday and not yours, I do not think I could bring myself to perform even the slightest of the many unreasonable activities that seem to be the normal method of celebration.

"For one thing, Vulcans do not voluntarily pollute their bloodstream with odd combinations of ethyl alcohol molecules." That seemed to outrage the chief and he drew back in stunned disbelief.

"Pollute? Mr. Flock, do I understand you to be sayin' . . . ? Are you callin' . . . ? Do you mean to say that you regard this outstandin' eggnog as a *pollutant*?"

"I believe that is what I just said, Mr. Scott. Really, if you cannot see—"

"No. No, that's all right, Block, I see. I see, all right." He shoved his chin out and managed to look like a Scottish martyr. He started gathering up armfuls of drawings. They overflowed his arms and fell to the floor. When he bent over to retrieve those that had fallen, he lost another set.

"If that's the way you feel about it," he continued, picking up one and dropping three, "I'll just have to find someone else to share this with. Someone who can appre-

ciate my design. Someone who'll be happy to share the in-
come."

Apparently deciding he'd reached the point of dimin-
ishing returns as far as dropped papers were concerned,
he turned and staggered off in the direction of a knot of
nearby subengineers, dripping diagrams all the way. The
subengineers saw him coming, but couldn't get out of the
way fast enough.

Spock watched him go. A hand touched his shoulder,
and he turned 'round, looking up at the new arrival.

"Hello, Captain." Spock's first worry—that he might
find the *Enterprise*'s commanding officer in a state similar
to that of its chief engineer—was unfounded. On the contrary, Kirk's face was noticeably devoid of seasonal spirit.
His current expression was a mixture of curiosity and puzzlement.

"Something is happening?"

Kirk nodded. "It's probably nothing important, Mr.
Spock. As you know, meteor activity has been unusually
heavy in this sector for two days now. This morning, Sulu
thought he'd detected a blip in the normal shower pattern
that shouldn't have been there. I checked his readings and
the computer seems to confirm them. There's something
moving in the shower that's acting very unmeteorlike.

"Still, it may be nothing more than a somewhat different hunk of cosmic flotsam—but it's drifting in a course
almost parallel to ours. Since it's not out of our way, I
told Sulu to veer toward it."

"Any idea what it might be, Captain?"

Kirk looked skeptical. "Sulu thinks it might be a ship."

"You have of course considered our position?"

Kirk nodded. "I know we're on the edge of the Romulan Neutral Zone, Mr. Spock. If it is a ship, there's the
chance it might be Romulan. Regardless—" He glanced
around the lounge, in which the noise level had risen
several unsteady decibels in the last few minutes, "if you
can spare a moment away from the local hilarity, I'd appreciate your presence on the bridge."

"I assure you, Captain, I can spare a great deal more
than a moment."

Spock continued his thoughts as they started moving toward the bridge-elevator.

"In fact, sometimes, Captain," and he looked back to where Ensign Burns was now chasing Uhura around the tree, "I often wonder how you humans ever managed to discover fire." Kirk hit the elevator switch, and they entered the lift.

"Sometimes, Mr. Spock, we aren't quite sure ourselves." He nudged the lever that sent them rising toward the bridge.

Spock said nothing for a while as the lights indicating other decks flashed past. But Kirk knew his first officer well enough to tell that something was digging at him.

"What is it, Spock?"

"An absurdity, Captain. It is merely that Engineer Scott was forcing me to look at plans for . . ." He paused awkwardly in midsentence, something he rarely did.

"Captain, do you think there would be much of a market on human-populated worlds for a four-dimensional Christmas tree?"

"A what? Mr. Spock, have you been . . . ?"

"Captain, I do not object to the diverse ingredients included in the liquid solution known as eggnog . . . though I find many of them frivolous rather than nutritional. But please rest assured the beverage itself has no attraction for me.

"Besides, I believe I may be allergic to nutmeg."

Kirk lost the answer to Spock's original question in the atmosphere of this rarified possibility.

Mr. Sulu was the only officer at station on the bridge. On special occasions Kirk sometimes allowed the *Enterprise* to cruise free, operating on the reasonable theory that no one had yet found a way to get a computer drunk. Sulu would have his own chance at losing control of himself when the starship changed over to the next shift.

For now, the helmsman's full attention was focused on his fore scanners.

"We're coming up on the object now, Captain."

"How's shower activity, Mr. Sulu?" Kirk slipped easily into the command chair and Spock moved to the library computer station.

"Heavy, sir, but not abnormal. Our shields and deflectors are handling it easily." Concern was in his voice. "But from what I can read, that ship out there hasn't done nearly as well."

"It is a ship, then?"

"Yes, sir." He made a delicate adjustment to a control. "Should have it on the screen any second now."

The main viewscreen blurred, then cleared. Meteors that occasionally shot across the field of vision moved too fast to be seen, but the tiny craft centered in the viewfinder stood out sharply in amplified starlight.

Its design was compact and very expensive. Only the very rich could afford to put warp-drive engines in small ships. That maxim held true for governments as well as individuals.

Right now, however, the ship looked more like a prime candidate for the scrapyard. The rear section had been twisted and bent in places by some violent, overwhelming force. The engines weren't twisted or bent because they weren't there anymore. The whole power plant was missing, torn from the stern of the battered craft.

Numerous gaping holes showed in the mid- and foresections as well. It was a choice hunk of junk.

"Take us in closer, Mr. Sulu."

"Aye, sir."

Matching velocity and direction with care, the helmsman edged the *Enterprise* close to the small vessel. It was a feat made possible only with the aid of the starship's navigational computer. No human could handle so many complex calculations alone.

"It's not a Romulan, anyway," Kirk muttered. He was mildly relieved. Realistically, aiding a distressed craft could in no way be interpreted as warlike. Not by humans or Vulcans, anyway. But the Romulans were not always realistic. They had some peculiar ideas as to what constituted an aggressive act. At least Kirk would be spared that worry. Instead he could concentrate his thoughts on the plight of the survivors, if any.

He didn't have to consult the computer records to see that the tiny craft was of Federation design and make. "Close scan, Mr. Sulu."

Sulu touched a switch. Immediately the rear section of the injured ship seemed to jump out at them. Moving slowly forward along the pitted fuselage, the telescopic scanner finally stopped on a set of identification numbers. Set just behind the living area, the glowing numbers were barely intelligible. A near-miss by a small chunk of iron-nickel had almost obliterated them.

"I have it, Captain," noted Spock. That was the signal for Sulu to move the scanner further along the side of the craft.

"I am now checking the number against Federation records." There was a short pause and then Spock added idly, "I might also say, Captain, that unless you are wrong and it *is* possible to induce a state of inebriation into computers, our sensors claim that at least one occupant of that ship is still alive."

Kirk's surprise was genuine. He hadn't really expected that a ship this badly hulled, drifting alone in a little-visited sector of space, might still be able to sustain life.

Still, they didn't know how long the vessel had been drifting helplessly or when its power plant had been destroyed. Its life-support systems could have been successfully sealed off from the rest of the damage and might have continued to function on stored emergency power, but— The state of the ship indicated otherwise.

Yet life-sensors rarely made mistakes.

Possibly someone else was due for a merry Christmas.

"Mr. Sulu. Since Lt. Uhura is . . . uh, otherwise engaged, I'd like you to try contacting that ship."

"Trying, sir," replied the helmsman, as he rerouted basic communications through his own board. There was a pause of several minutes, after which Sulu looked back and shook his head slowly.

"Nothing, sir. Not even a carrier wave. And no SOS."

Kirk tried to sound philosophical. "I guess it's too much to expect any of their communications equipment to have survived intact. Not after the beating she's taken. Your occupant may still be alive, Mr. Spock, but I wouldn't bet that he or she is in very good condition." He nudged a switch on his armrest.

"Sick Bay—Dr. McCoy, please. Captain calling." All that came back over the intercom was a muffled and suspiciously feminine giggle. "Bones, are you there?" An unidentifiable fumbling sound followed.

"Here, Jim. What's up?" Kirk suppressed an urge to echo McCoy's query and follow up his own curiosity. Instead he managed to concentrate on the problem at hand.

"Bones, we've run across a small Federation ship. It's a derelict, been through the mill, but according to our sensors at least one survivor is on board. We can't be sure yet. I'm going to have them beamed aboard, and you'd better be standing by in the transporter room."

"Okay, Jim." The giggle sounded again, and McCoy switched off—rather hurriedly, Kirk thought. He sighed, turned to Spock.

"Anything on the ship itself, yet?"

"Not yet, Captain. But we should have some information soon. I have already established that it is not a government vessel. Private listings of interstellar ships require rather more time to check thoroughly. I will join you and Dr. McCoy in the transporter room."

"All right, Spock."

McCoy was already waiting when Kirk arrived in the transporter chamber. The doctor was engaged in amiable conversation with Transporter Chief Kyle. Chatting ceased abruptly when Kirk entered and he had the impression their discussion had been on matters other than the derelict ship. McCoy struggled to put up a concerned front.

"Do we know anything about her yet, Jim?"

"Only that she is Federation, that she's probably privately owned, that in all likelihood she contains no more than one survivor, and fix your shirt."

McCoy looked down at himself and fumbled quickly with his clothing. Kirk nodded to the transporter chief.

"All right, Mr. Kyle," he ordered dryly. "The doctor is ready. Bring 'em aboard."

"Yes, sir."

A familiar musical whine started to rise in the room. Spock walked in and moved to stand between Kirk and McCoy as the transporter effect began to build.

"Readings indicate only one person aboard, Captain," informed Kyle. Kirk acknowledged.

"Thank you, Chief." He glanced at his first officer. "Have you identified her, Mr. Spock?"

"Yes, Captain," Spock replied quietly, keeping his eyes fixed on the reception alcove. Was there a hint of suppressed excitement in Spock's voice?

"You may find it difficult to believe—as difficult as I find it—but the vessel is registered to Carter Winston. I cross-checked, triple-checked. There is no mistake."

"The Carter Winston?"

Spock nodded once.

"That's impossible, Spock!" objected McCoy. He had recognized the name instantly, too. So had Kyle, but the transporter chief was too busy to give vent to his disbelief.

Everyone knew what Carter Winston had been.

"Carter Winston's been missing and presumed dead for over five years."

"It is possible, Doctor," mused Spock unemotionally, "that he is no longer missing." Kirk gestured towards the alcove where the outline of a figure was building.

"We'll know in a minute, gentlemen."

The outline began to fill in, become solid. Gradually certain characteristics established themselves. The figure was bipedal, human, male. Effect solidified and the glowing mist became man. At the same time, Kyle deftly dropped the single remaining control lever all the way down and snapped off power.

No one spoke.

A simple coverall suit of rich brown wood colors clothed the man. Its top was inlaid with accenting gold thread. The garment was a mixture of the restrained and expensive. A lime-gold aura still surrounded him, the product of the life-support belt encircling his waist.

The new arrival looked them over briefly, then stepped off the platform and switched off his belt. The aura vanished. It was obvious that as a doctor, McCoy's presence was superfluous. The survivor looked none the worse for wear after what must have been, at its mildest, a devastating ordeal.

Physically he seemed untouched, not so much as a

scratch marring his attractive, famous features. Although now in his late thirties, his long absence had apparently not affected his athlete's body. After half a decade of non-existence he showed no signs of deprivation.

He smiled slightly—his famous smile.

"Incredible!" McCoy finally managed to stutter, breaking the silence. "It *is* him!"

"Carter Winston," Kirk murmured, in tones usually reserved for addressing Starfleet admirals. It was appropriate. The man standing so composedly before them was a legend. Dead legends are not supposed to come back to life. The men grouped in the transporter room could be permitted a little awe.

Winston bestowed a curious, bemused glance on each of them in turn. A second later he showed that there was nothing the matter with his vocal cords, either.

"It seems you gentlemen know me." Kirk stepped forward and shook his hand.

"There are few in the Federation who wouldn't recognize you, sir. Even after all this time. It's good to know you're no longer a piece of history."

"I'm Captain James Kirk, commanding this vessel. It's an honor to have you aboard the *Enterprise*." He gestured in turn to each of the others.

"My first officer, Mr. Spock. Dr. McCoy, senior medical officer—" McCoy stepped forward and shook hands exuberantly.

"I'm especially honored to meet you, Mr. Winston. I expect your being alive means more to me than to the others. You see," he hesitated slightly, "my daughter was going to school on Cerberus ten years ago, when the crop failure occurred."

"Ah, yes," Winston murmured, "Cerberus."

McCoy looked over at Kirk, then back at Winston.

"It was estimated that fifty to sixty percent of the population would have starved if Winston, here, hadn't used his—well, you remember the stories.

"Bureaucracy in the Cerberus Crisis moved at two speeds—dead slow and slower than dead. But Winston spent his personal fortune to bring in enough food and goods to carry the Cerberus II inhabitants through the danger period until those idiots," and he spoke the word with as much bitterness as Kirk had ever heard from him, "at Administration got themselves straightened out."

Kirk recalled the incident faintly and was impressed with the memory. He wasn't as intimately acquainted with the Cerberus incident as McCoy, but he remembered some of the resulting tremors. There had been a real shakeup in certain sections of Starfleet Command. One of those rare instances where ministers and executives in high positions actually lost their jobs.

"One of the many stories I've heard about you, Mr. Winston. It's a great pleasure for all of us to see you alive and well."

"Thank you, gentlemen." Winston smiled again, the same infectious grin that had more than once graced broadcast screens from the Far Arm to Earth itself—and had helped to build one of the greatest if most unstable fortunes of all time.

"I'd like to say it's a pleasure to be on the *Enterprise,* but frankly, after what I've been through these last five years, it'd be a pleasure to be on board a pressurized bathtub."

The four humans shared a convivial laugh. Spock waited and watched impatiently. There were a couple of things he badly wanted to say, and he had held his peace while jovial greetings had been exchanged.

"There is one person aboard who will be especially glad to learn that you are alive—Lieutenant Anne Nored of our Security Section."

Winston kept his composure, but not enough to hide the shock he obviously felt.

"My fiancée! Anne's aboard this ship?"

"Yes, doesn't it please you?"

McCoy broke in before an astonished Winston had a chance to reply. "How did you know that, Mr. Spock?"

"As soon as it was determined that the craft we located was registered to Mr. Winston, I began processing information on him on the chance that he was the lone survivor. The information concerning his engagement to Lieutenant Nored was in the capsule summary the computer produced. It is a surprise to me too, doctor." He turned back to Winston.

"We will notify her as soon as we have verified and processed your credentials, sir. If you have your identity tapes with you . . . ?"

"Spock!" McCoy looked angry. "Of all the cold-blooded, inhospitable and inhuman requests I've ever heard—"

"I believe the regulations are quite clear on the matter, Doctor," replied a composed Spock. "An immediate identity check and full medical examination are standard procedure in situations such as this. Despite the unusual nature of the rescue, I find no reason for deviating from procedure."

McCoy clearly felt otherwise and seemed prepared to say so. But Kirk, after a questioning glance at Spock, moved quickly to ease the awkward moment.

"Spock's right, Bones. Be sensible."

McCoy hesitated and still looked upset, but said nothing.

"And I understand, of course," smiled Winston. "My credentials, Captain." He reached into a suit pocket and withdrew a small microtape cassette. Kirk gave it a curious, cursory glance. Tape models had changed slightly in five years. If nothing else, the cassette Winston held out to him was genuine as to age.

"We'll get through the formalities as rapidly as possible, Mr. Winston. Bones, why don't you take our guest down to Sick Bay and run him through a standard medical check."

McCoy nodded, smiled at Winston. "I was going to suggest a twelve-course meal first, but it *would* be a good idea to make sure your insides are in shape to appreciate it. I'll make it fast, Mr. Winston."

The two men left the chamber, chatting excitedly. McCoy was doing most of the talking as the elevator doors slid together in front of them, but that didn't surprise Kirk. After all, a man can miss a lot of news in five years.

"Five years! It's still hard to believe, Spock."

"I know, Captain." The two officers turned into the

small briefing room. It was the nearest place to the transporter chamber that had the proper computer-access module.

"Nonetheless, he produced his identity tapes immediately. His actions so far have been perfectly normal. Oh, maybe he's a bit composed for someone who's been out of touch with civilization for five years, but—"

"It is a part of his character. Yes, Captain, everything seems to indicate that he is, indeed, Carter Winston."

"We'll know in a minute." Kirk took a seat at the briefing table and activated a small switch set into the compact console in front of him.

"Ship's log, please." There was a short pause, then a soft beep indicating that the computer had recognized his voice and would now deign to record. Kirk spoke into the small grid set into the tabletop.

"Captain's log, supplemental. The *Enterprise* has rescued a living legend—the foremost interstellar trader of our time, Carter Winston. Who, as I recall, has acquired a dozen fortunes, only to use his great wealth again and again to aid Federation colonies in times of need or disaster.

"Altogether a remarkable man and one who many people, myself included, are glad to discover is still alive. We are in the process of carrying out standard postrescue identification procedures." He hit another switch, then slipped the microtape cassette into a slot that had suddenly appeared in the desk.

"Library computer—process identification tapes on male human known as Carter Winston. Verification of identity requested." A three-sided viewscreen popped out of the desk top. It immediately displayed a set of fingerprints in triplicate. These were followed in rapid succession by a series of retinal patterns, oscilloscope readings, and other information.

"Working," informed the slightly feminine machine voice. There was a muted hum.

"Identification positive," it finally declaimed. Kirk gave an inward sigh. Of *course*, it was Carter Winston! The need for Spock's logical mind to cross *t*'s and dot *i*'s had made him overcautious.

The computer continued. "Identification confirmation follows: fingerprints positive, voiceprints positive, retinal relief positive. All registration and documentation in order."

"Original visual display, please." The abstracts disappeared to be replaced by a hologram of Winston. Except for a few touches Kirk quickly ascribed to normal aging, it differed in no way from the man they had beamed aboard. An extra line here, a slight softening of flesh there. Both men studied the 'gram for another minute. Then Kirk hit the switch, and the tripartite screen sank back into the table.

He leaned back in the chair and gazed across the table at his first officer. "Well, everything checks out. So we have a distinguished passenger for a while. I expect he won't exactly be a dull guest—ought to have one or two stories to tell."

"It would seem so, Captain. I am much relieved."

"You worry too much, Spock. And now, if you'll excuse me—" Kirk moved briskly out of the chair. "It's time for me to go and pollute myself with exotic combinations of protein solids and ethanol molecules."

"*Et tu*, Captain? You were listening."

Kirk only grinned as they exited the briefing room.

II

"If you'll just lie down over there," requested McCoy, indicating the nearby examination table. Winston hopped up on the slightly tilted platform. With the air of one thoroughly enjoying a relaxed position, he stretched out and put both hands under his head.

McCoy walked to a nearby cabinet and selected a compact general scanner.

"This won't hurt a bit, Winston," he said easily as he

moved to stand next to the table. "Just a few minutes and we'll be all through." He smiled, flicked a switch on the scanner. Starting at the top of Winston's head, McCoy moved the instrument down the man's body, holding it roughly ten centimeters above him.

After passing over his feet, McCoy flicked the device off and checked the readouts. His smile slipped away and was replaced by a slight frown of puzzlement.

Winston noticed it, too. "Is there some problem, Doctor? Don't tell me—I'm pregnant!"

McCoy managed a smile. "Scanner seems a little off. Just a second." He adjusted dials, rechecked the readouts. "Calibration must be off," he muttered to himself. He nudged the activation switch again and played the pickup over his own upper torso, examined the results. His puzzlement deepened.

Mumbling with the air of someone who's just seen a ghost and prefers to pretend it wasn't really there, he turned back to Winston.

"Let's try it again."

Once more the scanner was played down the survivor's prone form. Once more the resultant numbers on the tiny gauges brought deepening confusion.

"Odd. Some slight deviations here and there I could understand. You've been isolated for five years. It's no surprise that your body might have picked up some funny radiation, or something. A couple of abnormal readings are to be expected. It's just that . . ." he looked down at Winston with a worried stare, "I've never gotten any readings quite like these from a human being before."

Winston laughed easily, clearly amused by McCoy's confusion. "Are you suggesting I'm not quite human, doctor? By the way, Merry Christmas."

"Merry Christmas to you, Winston. No, of course not. Anyway, the differences are all fractional." His smile returned. "Sometimes even the best medical instrumentation goes haywire. I don't get to overhaul it with major hospital facilities very often. Must be the scanner."

"Occasionally the transporter can do peculiar things to a body, too, leaving lingering effects that disappear as the internal structure readjusts. How are you feeling?"

Winston spread his hands, looked bemused. "Just great, Doc."

"Well, then—"

"I beg your pardon, Dr. McCoy." The doctor turned. Nurse Chapel had stepped into the examination room from the nearby reception area.

"What is it, Christine?"

"Doctor, the captain has been calling. He wants to know if the examination has been completed."

"Ummm, yes, I suppose it has."

"And doctor, Lt. Nored is waiting to see Mr. Winston—as soon as you've certified his medical status."

"Thanks, Christine." She smiled and left. McCoy turned back to Winston. "Well, I certainly don't want to keep you from your fiancée." He turned and yelled towards the open door. "Send her in, Christine."

He offered Winston a last smile, one he also shared with the woman who passed him in the doorway.

She was dressed in the red uniform of a senior security officer. Not stunning, no, but she was damned attractive in an unassuming sort of way. As befitted a security officer, she was in excellent physical shape, which was more than could be said for her state of mind just then.

"Carter—"

She held herself pretty well in check until she was almost to him. Then her reserve cracked and she threw herself into his arms. Caught off-balance, his arms went around her automatically as he stumbled.

His own reaction was considerably less emotional. Calm, cool, and—something else. Something as yet undefinable.

She was alternately sobbing and talking a blue streak. He let her ramble on for several minutes before moving his hands up to her shoulders and pushing her gently away—gently, but firmly.

"I'm sorry, Anne." The sorrow in his voice seemed genuine. "I never thought we would meet again."

She studied his face. As she did so, her expression changed from one of relief and pleasure to one of confused uncertainty.

"What is it, Carter? What's the matter?" Winston replied without hesitation.

"When I left on that final journey, Anne, I fully intended it to be my last. One supreme foray into unknown regions to bring my finances back to where they'd been before. After that, I would return and marry you. But my ship was disabled, and I crashed on the planet Vendor. I'm told I was lucky to have survived at all. The Vendorians managed to help me repair my ship. I left their world after four years of hard work, only to be disabled in space once again."

"But you've been rescued, you've survived," she almost shouted. "You're alive and we're together again! Nothing's changed." Winston looked away from her.

"Anne, I've changed. First there was the surgery—a lot of surgery. Skin grafts, bone regeneration, replacement of damaged organs with artificial ones, blood replacement. The Vendorians are excellent surgeons." He smiled slightly at some distant memory. "They said I was more banged up than the ship.

"After they put me back together again, the Vendorians assigned one of their own people to look after me and nurse me back to health."

All this was very interesting—fascinating, even—but it did nothing to explain Winston's original statement.

"But you said you've changed, Carter. How? I don't see any change."

"It's not a visible kind of change, Anne. It's a kind that—" He paused. Abruptly he seemed to give up any attempt at further explanation.

"It's over between us, Anne. I can't really explain why, or how, but it's *over*. I didn't expect to have to go through this. All I can say now that it's happened is that I can't marry you, ever." He continued to watch her quietly.

Her mouth moved but no sounds came out. Everything had happened so suddenly and seemingly so well. Even his first bits of explanation appeared to leave room for hope. Then he had abruptly grown firm and inflexible, hitting her with a declaration as blunt and cold as the dark side of the moon.

She turned and ran from the room, leaving Winston sitting alone on the cold examination table, staring after her.

Kirk had performed the ceremonial gesture of drinking with the crew—sharing their spirits, so to speak. But he'd returned to the bridge soon enough. Now he was back in the command chair, using a light-writer to mark orders on a glass plate lined with metal. A young yeoman, Ayers, stood to one side, awaiting the captain's bidding.

Nodding in satisfaction, he read back over the orders, signed the plate and handed it to her.

"See these are delivered to the proper stations and processed through, Yeoman." Ayers saluted and left the bridge.

A slight wave of dizziness assailed Kirk. He put a hand to his forehead. Possibly he'd overdone the annual Christmas camaraderie. He might be better off in his cabin for a while. It was one thing for the general crew to wander around mildly dazed during the holidays, but the captain was expected to remain cold sober at all times—in public, anyway.

"Take the conn, Mr. Spock. I'll be in my cabin, completing the report on Winston's rescue."

"Very good, Captain."

Kirk rose and headed for the bridge-elevator. Spock shifted from the library station and took over the command chair.

Kirk thought about the report as he made his way from the second elevator to his private quarters. He was still thinking about it after he'd kicked off his shoes and sat down at his desk. His finger activated the recorder, but for long moments he just sat and considered, unable to find anything to say. It was all so incredible, so utterly impossible.

Five years completely out of touch with civilization! And who knew how much of that had been spent drifting free in space, without another human being for company.

Oh, there were records of people surviving even longer periods of time adrift. The trouble was never with their bodies, but with their minds. Yet Winston seemed as sane and composed when he'd stepped out of the transporter as if he'd been gone only a day or two.

Kirk shook his head in admiration. It had always been said the man was a remarkable person. Plenty of stories testified to it—the Cerberus incident being only one of many—and now Kirk knew it from personal experience.

He was about to start dictating when the door chime demanded his attention.

"Come—"

The door slid back silently, and Winston walked in.

"I hope I'm not intruding, Captain?"

"No, please come in, Mr. Winston. I was just about to finish off the official report on your rescue." He grinned. "When Starfleet makes the details available, the news people will go crazy. You're liable to be faxed to death the moment you set foot on Federation soil."

"I expect as much." Winston smiled back. "I've been down to inspect my ship. Your people were kind enough to stow it in the shuttle bay. You know, the steering propulsors still operate. Remarkable."

Kirk turned away, hunting for the microtape analysis of Winston's ship. "Yes, it's an understatement to say the ship suffered severe damage. It'll never travel at warp-speed again, but some of the systems still function and are salvageable. And there are all your expensive fittings to consider."

"Anyway, I've had my chief engineer examine it thoroughly and draw up a full report for you. It's here somewhere—"

Winston crossed his arms over his chest. There was nothing particularly unusual in the gesture.

The results were otherwise.

His outline seemed to flutter, to blur, and then to flow like a thin, phosphorescent clay. The flow slowed, stopped.

Where Winston had stood now rose a hideous, multicolored something. It had seven thick tentacles which met at the top and merged to form an oval bulge encircled with convex lenses. The lenses pulsed with faint light.

One of the tentacles lifted from the floor. It touched Kirk gently, almost caressingly, on the back of the neck. The captain's eyes closed. Other tentacles moved to catch the slumping form. The creature lifted the unconscious Kirk and carried him effortlessly to the bed. Only a few seconds had passed from transformation to attack, and everything had been done in complete silence.

Now the thing stepped back from the bed and crossed a pair of tentacles over its upper body—it had no recognizable chest. Again the blur, the watery flow. Once more the creature changed and became human.

It didn't become Carter Winston.

But it was human, nonetheless, and immediately recognizable.

It was Captain James T. Kirk.

Nurse Chapel entered the examination room from the laboratory area and moved to where Dr. McCoy sat engrossed in detailed inspection of a medical-engineering manual. She held the small hand scanner in one hand and several smaller supplementary instruments in the other. McCoy glanced up from his reading.

"Well, Christine?"

"Doctor," she said firmly, "I can't find a single thing wrong with these instruments. They all check out perfectly, including the principal scanner. But the readings still come out slightly off, still show those funny variations on Winston." She watched him expectantly.

"What about the other tests you ran on Winston, after—" She hesitated. Two things travel faster than the speed of light—starships and gossip. Romantic gossip fastest of all.

McCoy shrugged. Some things were impossible to keep secret. "After Anne Nored left? Some of them were off, some weren't. The differences don't even have the virtue of consistency, Christine. As it stands, these results make no sense at all. It's got to be our mistake." He stood.

"Come on. We'll evaluate those readings again, and this time we're going to find the answer."

The elevator doors opened onto the bridge, and Winston/Kirk entered. Spock looked back at him and rose from the command chair. Winston/Kirk took the seat as the first officer returned to his own station.

Sulu glanced back at the command chair with interest. "Weren't you going to your cabin, sir?"

"I've already been there, Mr. Sulu, but something came up before I could get started on the report. Something much more important. Lay on a direct course for Rator III." That prompted another look, this time of more than just casual interest.

"Through the Romulan Neutral Zone, sir?"

"That was an order, Helmsman."

Sulu looked uncertain. "But sir, if we're challenged in there, the Romulans can confiscate the ship. The treaty states that—"

"I am fully conversant with the terms of the treaty, Mr. Sulu," responded Winston/Kirk, "and I believe you heard my order."

"Aye aye, sir," the helmsman admitted reluctantly. He turned to the task of plotting the requested course.

Spock, who had listened to this exchange with growing concern, finally felt obliged to at least say something cautionary. He wasn't normally in the habit of raising objections to any of Kirk's decisions, no matter how strange they sounded at first, because they always seemed to have a way of turning out to be reasonable in the end.

But this one. Spock made a last check of his console. The readings confirmed his suspicions.

"Captain, extreme long-range sensors hint at something within the neutral zone that lies along our anticipated course. At this exaggerated distance it is impossible to determine what it is. It might be another interstellar merchant ship like Winston's. It might also be a Romulan vessel. Or it might not be a ship at all. Still I do not feel it prudent to take the chance of trespassing unannounced in the neutral zone."

"Mr. Spock," replied Winston/Kirk, "I've spoken with Winston about this at some length already. He has assured me that it is absolutely vital to get to Rator III in the shortest possible time. The survival of an entire planetary population may depend on it. Unfortunately, this necessitates our crossing through an arm of the neutral zone."

"An admirable mission, Captain," Spock agreed. "But

if we endanger our ship, we will be of no use to the people on Rator III."

"We won't be of any use to them if we don't get there in time, either, Mr. Spock. I wouldn't have ordered it if I didn't feel it was safe to proceed. Winston said his sensors detected no sign of Romulans when he was passing through the zone, before his ship was disabled. I'm satisfied he was telling the truth. And his word is considered good, isn't it?"

Spock hesitated a split second. "That has been his reputation, Captain."

"Course laid in, sir," Sulu noted.

"Execute," ordered Winston/Kirk. Sulu leaned forward and adjusted controls.

"Proceeding."

They felt no sense of motion-change. Space was too vast for inbuilt human senses to detect a switch in direction at warp-speeds. But the great starship gradually began to veer from the line it had been following and to turn in a broad curve that would take it into the neutral zone.

Sulu needed only a few moments to double-check his readings.

"We're on course, sir."

"Very good, Mr. Sulu. Notify me if anything unusual should develop." He rose and moved towards the elevator. "I'm going back to my cabin. You have the conn again, Mr. Spock."

Spock eyed the captain closely as the latter exited the bridge.

Time passed. Nothing happened to disturb ship routine, which was perfectly all right with Spock. After some hard thinking, he finally thumbed the switch activating the ship's log and spoke softly into the pickup grid.

"Ship's log, stardate 5402.7. First Officer Spock recording.

"The captain's recent course change has taken us deep into the Romulan Neutral Zone. This change was apparently initiated on the request of our new passenger, Carter Winston. Information so far provided by Winston has proved accurate. We have detected no Romulan ships or, for that matter, other vessels of any kind.

"Nevertheless, I have ordered all sensors kept on long-range scan and a close watch on any object engendering suspicion at the limits of scanner range. I have also . . ."

Dizzy, he was still dizzy.

Kirk winced and sat up suddenly in bed. Two things struck him right away. First of all, he hadn't had that much to drink. And eggnog had never, never had that kind of effect on him. He'd imbibed a lot of liquids quite a sight stronger than the holiday punch, which was pablum by comparison. None of them had ever hit him like *this*!

And besides that—

He glanced over at the chronometer set into the wall above his bed. Uh-uh, something was wrong with that, too. What had happened?

Think back. Sometimes it was better to voice confusing thoughts in the presence of others. *He* couldn't figure out what had happened to him. Maybe someone else could.

Kirk strode purposefully onto the bridge. Though he was feeling terribly confused, there was no point in letting anyone else know it, just yet.

"I'll take the conn, Mr. Spock." Spock lifted an eyebrow slightly but moved away without comment. Sulu also glanced back at him curiously.

Kirk sat back in the seat, relaxed, and tried very hard to remember. Introspection produced nothing, but a casual glance forward turned up an interesting node of information indeed.

His gaze touched on the big chronometer on the navigation console, the one that set ship-time for the rest of the *Enterprise*. It read 1405.

There was nothing world smashing in that. However, he distinctly remembered the time on his wall chronometer as he was leaving his cabin. 1404, it said. And when he'd been searching his desk for a certain cassette before—before falling asleep—he'd happened to notice the time on the desk timepiece.

It had read 1400.

Not shockingly significant, perhaps, but—

Spock, who'd been watching Kirk indirectly ever since

the other had returned to the bridge, noticed Kirk's confusion.

"Is something wrong, Captain?"

"I'm not . . . I'm not sure, Spock."

"Do you feel all right, sir?" This from an alarmed Sulu.

"Fine, Mr. Sulu, just fine. But am I?" He turned to
Spock, mumbled half to himself, "I'd gone back to my
quarters to dictate the rest of the rescue report ... I
remember that much. And I seem ... to have fallen
asleep. But the odd thing is, Mr. Spock, I can't recall
moving from my desk to the bed. And I can't ever
remember falling asleep so quickly—and so soundly—for
just a few minutes.

"If I was as tired as all that, it seems I ought to have
slept an hour or so."

"Possibly you needed the rest more than you think,
Captain," suggested Spock, having no conclusions yet to
jump to. "The body has its own system of checks and bal-
ances in that regard. You obviously required only the
briefest of naps."

"In any case, nothing has changed since you left. We're
still on course through the neutral zone to Rator III."

"But I don't remember going to—" Kirk stopped,
looked at Spock in sudden amazement as his last words
penetrated. "The Romulan Neutral Zone?"

"It is the only neutral zone we were near, Captain," the
first officer replied with gentle irony.

"I gave no authorization to enter it, Mr. Spock. Did
you order a course change?"

"No, sir," Spock replied, now equally confused. "You
did."

"Ridiculous!" Kirk's mind was spinning. First a highly
unnatural nap, and now Spock seemed to have gone
crazy. Or maybe he was still asleep and this was all a bad
dream.

If so, it was long past time for him to wake up.

"No one in Starfleet would issue such an order unless
it was a matter of life and death, Spock."

"I believe that was the rationale you employed, Captain." He turned and moved a toggle switch on the instru-

ment panel above his head. There was a small screen set into the panel. Both he and Kirk stared at it.

The screen came to life, and the scene that had taken place on the bridge only moments before was repeated.

"Weren't you going to your cabin, sir?" intoned a recorded Sulu as Kirk watched incredulously.

"I've already been there, Mr. Sulu ... set a direct course for Rator III."

"Through the Romulan Neutral Zone, sir?"

"That was an order, Helmsman."

Kirk turned away from the damning screen. He'd had enough. More than enough. "That will do, Spock." Spock obligingly shut off the recording and swiveled to face his captain.

Kirk leaned back in the chair, very thoughtful. A number of explanations suggested themselves. As he examined each one and moved on to the next, they grew progressively outrageous and less and less realistic.

One thing he did know, though. Until this was all worked out and a reasonable explanation *did* suggest itself, he had to get off the bridge.

"Mr. Sulu, locate Mr. Scott and have him report to the bridge to take command, please." He rose and headed towards the exit. Spock moved to accompany him.

"Also, Mr. Sulu," he said back over his shoulder, "plot a course to take the *Enterprise* out of the neutral zone at warp-six. Lt. M'ress, put the ship on yellow alert."

"Cerrtainly, Captain," acknowledged the concerned lieutenant.

"Yellow alert, sir?" wondered Spock as the doors joined behind them.

"I think it's necessary, Spock, until I can get a handle on this situation. I don't feel in a position to take any chances ... with whatever's going on here. Surely by now you've noticed that both my actions and my orders of the past hour have been, well, contradictory."

"I confess that something of the sort had occurred to me, Captain. But the reasons why—"

"Mr. Spock," Kirk's voice was grim, "I don't remember giving those orders to enter the neutral zone. I left the bridge, went to my cabin, fell asleep for a few moments, and returned to the bridge. That's all."

As usual, Spock's logic took precedence over tact, though Kirk didn't notice. He wanted answers, not sympathy. Too many vital things were at stake.

"Perhaps it would be a good idea to have Dr. McCoy examine you, Captain?"

"I agree absolutely. If I've become subject to mental blackouts, let alone physical ones, during which I give dangerous orders, then I've become a danger to the ship. I can't begin to imagine what's happened to me, but I can't take chances with a possibility like that."

He hit a switch, and the elevator lights shifted from vertical to horizontal. They were now moving down the length of the *Enterprise*.

It still didn't add up.

The instruments themselves continued to check out, efficiency bordered on a hundred percent, and yet they persisted in coughing up the same ridiculous readings. McCoy muttered to himself, bent for the umpteenth time to try to correlate the numbers on the scanner with those in a printed table of fine print glowing on a small readout screen.

The door chimed and he didn't look back. The figure of Carter Winston walked into the examination room. It watched patiently as McCoy continued matching figures that didn't match the way they were supposed to. Eventually McCoy glanced irritably to see who had entered. When he recognized Winston, he smiled a quick greeting before returning to his work.

"Hello, Winston," he said while running a new set of figures across the screen. "Still trying to figure this out. Sometimes I wonder if I shouldn't have taken more Instrumentation in med school."

So intent was McCoy on his study that he failed to notice the transformation behind him—a transformation that would have confused his instruments a good deal more.

He didn't see Winston place his arms over his chest, didn't see him dissolve like instant pudding and become a strange alien apparition, one that glided across the smooth floor on thick appendages with the grace of a ballerina.

"Winston, I've been over your tests two dozen times, and I don't think——" A tentacle rose, touched the back of McCoy's neck. The doctor slumped in his seat.

The alien thing caught him easily and carried him into the adjoining laboratory. As it placed the doctor on the floor, the sound of the examination-room door could be heard operating.

Anne Nored peered into the deserted room. "Dr. McCoy?" She took a step inside and the door automatically closed behind her. "Dr. McCoy?"

In the lab, the creature made motions with its tentacles. Seconds later a duplicate Dr. McCoy was standing over the limp form of the original. Anne Nored walked over to McCoy's workbench. She idly examined the scanner and the other devices McCoy had been pouring over without touching any of them. There was a slight shuffling sound and she jerked to her right.

"Dr. McCoy, you startled me."

Winston/McCoy stepped out of the lab, making sure the door closed behind him. "Nothing startles you, Anne, you're a security officer, and one of the best. Can I help you?"

"Oh, all right, so I was role playing." She smiled, but it faded quickly to an expression of awkwardness. "I thought this might be easy, doctor, but it's not. I don't know if you can . . . I just thought . . . well, I have to talk to somebody. And the other gals," she smiled a little again, "have a tendency to be less than serious about such things. I'd like to laugh at it, too, but I can't. It hurts too much. So I thought maybe you . . . ?"

Winston/McCoy seemed to hesitate, then gestured to a chair. Anne sat down gratefully. When she didn't seem able to continue, Winston/McCoy spoke.

"Let me guess. It's about you and Carter Winston." He paused for a moment, added, "He told me a little about it when I was examining him."

"How much is 'a little,' doctor?" Again Winston/McCoy appeared to pause.

"Enough."

"Doctor, what am I going to do?" she finally blurted desperately. "I know you're not a psychiatrist, and I don't think I need that. I'm not mentally unbalanced. I don't think, but I still love him." The corners of her mouth twisted upwards a little.

"Come to think of it, love is classified by some as a state of temporary mental unbalance, isn't it?"

"Only by poets, writers of romantic fiction, and the French," Winston/McCoy replied. He turned and focused his attention on the blank wall opposite.

"I'm sure he'd like to feel the same way about you, Anne. He also told me something of the times you two had together, of the experiences you shared. Not a great deal, but I think I can understand the depth of feeling you had for each other.

"But it all may be impossible to recapture, Anne. Five years can be forever to someone. People change. People in love more frequently than most. And one thing I can tell you with assurance—Carter Winston's been through changes no other human being ever experienced." His voice dropped and he murmured, "Yes, people change."

"Well, I haven't!" she finally shouted. "What am I supposed to do? What *can* I do?"

"If he asked you to forget him," said Winston/McCoy, "I think you should try to do just that. Or would you prefer that he lie to you, tell you what you want to hear, intentionally deceive you. Do you want him to do that?"

"Oh, no. He's the gentlest, most thoughtful man I've ever known. Ever will know. And I don't think he could carry it off very well. Lying's not in his nature."

"Well, then, you see?" Winston/McCoy insisted. "If he doesn't want you any longer, for whatever reasons, and he's asked you to forget him, then all I can do is suggest that you take that as an honest concern for you and do it."

"You have no knowledge of what he's been through, of what—" and Winston/McCoy half smiled,—"unusual changes may have taken place in the years he's been gone. As a physician I can only advise you . . . and also as a friend. Forget Winston."

"Forget Carter—" The words came without any force,

any conviction behind them. She seemed ready to argue further, but the door chimed. Kirk and Spock entered. It was hard enough to articulate such intimate feelings in front of the ship's doctor. It would be impossible in front of the ship's captain and first officer.

So instead of continuing, she stood. "Thank you, Doctor McCoy. I'll consider your advice."

"Do that, Anne . . . Lieutenant Nored."

Kirk studied the security officer as she left, then turned to Winston/McCoy. The doctor smiled pleasantly.

"What can I do for you, Jim?"

"Bones, I need a complete medical examination."

"On Carter Winston? But I've already—" Kirk waved him off impatiently.

"No, no. For myself. Something's just happened that—" He stopped. The figure of Winston/McCoy had abruptly turned away from him and was now engaged in studying a microtape index file mounted on the far wall.

"I'm afraid I'll have to make it later in the day, Captain. I have too many tests to process right now."

Kirk had too many thoughts whirling through his head to react to that, but Spock looked puzzled. Being the favorite target of McCoy's brash wit, maybe he was more sensitive to the doctor's moods—or changes in personality.

"Carter Winston's, for example?" Spock inquired. Winston/McCoy half-turned, but didn't look at them.

"No, that one's done, completed. No trouble at all, Mr. Spock. Standard tests run, checked out completely normal."

"Are you sure there's no possibility you made an error?" persisted Spock.

Now it was Kirk's turn to look questioningly at his first officer instead of vice versa. It wasn't like Spock to question another officer's work—especially McCoy's. But it would be like McCoy—almost required of him—to respond with some especially devastating remark.

Instead, the doctor only chuckled. "Well, there's always that chance. I'll go over them again, if you like."

"No, that won't be necessary, Bones. I'll drop by later

for that examination, when you're not so busy. Let's go, Spock." Kirk turned and started for the door.

When it was securely shut behind them and they were out in the empty reception room, both men stopped and exchanged uncertain looks.

"Captain, did you notice Dr. McCoy's reaction when I asked him if there was a possibility he might have made an error in Carter Winston's tests?"

Kirk nodded.

"Yes. He didn't jump all over you when you questioned his accuracy. That isn't normal."

"Excuse me, Captain—'jump all over me?' "

"Said something along the lines of, 'there's as much chance of that as my falling down with . . .' "

" 'hysterical laughter at a joke of mine,' " finished Spock.

"Yes, that's it. What's even less normal is that he agreed with you. He conceded the chance, and that's not like Bones at all. If there's anything he's supremely confident about, it's his own competence as a physician. Come to think of it, it was also not like him to put off my request for a physical."

"I quite agree, Captain. Which means—"

"I don't know what it means," Kirk muttered, "except that maybe there are two officers on this ship who need medical checks. Come on!"

They burst into the Sick-Bay examination chamber and were dumbfounded at what they saw. Or rather, at what they didn't see.

The room was empty.

Neither officer feeling particularly bright at that moment, they moved to make a thorough search of the room.

"There is only one entrance to these inner medical rooms," mused Spock thoughtfully. "For security reasons, and for quarantine purposes. There are not a great many places a man could hide."

"No," agreed Kirk, "and I think—"

"Ohhhh . . ."

Kirk and Spock were at the entrance to the nearby lab in seconds. Both men were wary, expecting—they weren't sure what—to come charging pell-mell out at them. But the door slid back normally at Kirk's touch and nothing barred their entrance.

McCoy was sitting up in the middle of the floor, rubbing the side of his head. He looked very much as if he'd just absorbed a substantial dose of something a good deal stronger than eggnog.

"Bones?"

McCoy didn't react at first. Then he looked up at them, still dazed.

"Must have . . . must have fallen asleep . . . somehow, I guess. A little nap—"

"A little nap," echoed Kirk, reflecting on the similarity of a recent experience. "I think I have an idea what you mean, Bones."

"Doctor, you are a man of curious habits," observed Spock, "but I have never known you to nap on the laboratory floor. Elementary logic dictates that even an examination table would be far more comfortable, as well as—" He paused in midsentence at Kirk's raised hand. The captain was staring intently around the inner laboratory.

Ever since they'd entered he had not felt quite right about something. And not because of what they half expected to find—without knowing what it was. No, it was a feeling he still couldn't pin down. Spock would say it was illogical, but damn it, he felt *something* was wrong!

"Something is not right with this room."

McCoy made a rapid examination of his laboratory. His gaze returned eventually to Kirk's uncertain face.

"Everything looks okay to me, Jim."

"No," Kirk objected hurriedly. "Take a moment and think about it, Bones." Before McCoy could comment, the captain moved quickly to shut the door behind them.

"Both of you, study the room. There's definitely something different from the last time I was in here. I can't put my finger on it yet, but—"

The three officers started a patient, methodical survey of the laboratory. There didn't seem to be a great deal that might conceal some startling revelation. It didn't help that they had no idea what to look for, Kirk included.

Desks, wall decorations, shelves full of vials and tubes and neatly racked instruments, the gleaming surgical cases, emergency power chargers for use in case of ship-board power failure, the big portable sterilizer, three examination tables . . .

Even an examination table would be far more comfortable, Spock had said.

Kirk smiled then. "All right, Winston, you can come out now." Both Spock and McCoy turned their attention to the captain, Spock interestedly, McCoy incredulously.

Kirk walked forward until he was standing directly in front of the examination table farthest to the left. He spoke not behind it nor under it, but to it.

"I suggest you show yourself, Winston, or whatever you are. The masquerade's over."

Making no sense of the scene and getting no elucidation from Kirk, McCoy slowly got to his feet and whispered to Spock.

"Did you say that *I'm* a man of curious habits, Spock? Jim's talking to a table!"

"I don't think so, Doctor." An idea was beginning to solidify in the first officer's mind as he added certain known factors and proceeded toward a result. Evidently Kirk had already gotten there.

The captain stepped back from the table and turned his attention to one of the nearby wall shelves. Kirk spoke to the others as he studied the labels on the neat rows of crystal vials.

"There used to be only two examination tables in this room, as I recall, Bones." He focused his attention on the top row of containers. "Now there seem to be three."

Spock said nothing, but McCoy suddenly found himself nodding in agreement. "I just realized that too, Jim. But even so, what—" McCoy shut up. Whatever was happening here ought to come to a head pretty soon.

Kirk finally selected one of the smaller vials from the shelf. He walked back to stand next to the table.

The vial in his hand was made of thick, heat-formed artificial quartz alloyed with certain other metallic and ceramic components. It contained a small amount of thin purple fluid. When McCoy saw which vial the captain had removed he started forward, then stopped.

Again, Kirk directed his comments to the table. The

flat, unmistakably inorganic surface gleamed brightly in the overhead lights, small wheels and dials sparkling with polish. McCoy studied it till his eyes hurt, looking for some hidden sign he might have missed that would reveal the table's mysterious secrets to him.

It looked like an examination table. Kirk tapped it with one finger, and there was a faint ping.

It sounded like an examination table.

By Andromeda, it *was* an examination table!

"This is a vial of orientine acid," Kirk informed the table solemnly. "It will burn through just about anything but this holding crystal. If you've never seen it work, I'll be happy to demonstrate." He patted the table again. "On you."

There was a reasonable pause. Then Kirk raised the vial over the table and moved his thumb toward the cap release set into one side. The table shimmered suddenly, the sort of eye-tricking flutter of things seen out of one's corner of vision that aren't there anymore when you turn to look at them. The table rippled dreamily and changed form.

A moment later it was no longer an examination table. In its place stood a tall creature of thick, cabled limbs and shining eye lenses that stared back at them unwinkingly.

"I saw that," said a gaping McCoy," but I don't believe it."

"A Vendorian, Doctor," Spock informed him. "Their planet is quarantined, and few people ever see them. Their ability to rearrange their molecular structure at will to resemble anything of the same approximate mass—and their practice of deceit as a way of life—places them very much off-limits to others."

"Their unusual abilities could be of considerable value to the Federation, or to others. But as desirable as their physical attributes might be, psychologically they are still unfit for participation in a community of worlds.

"Mr. Spock, get a security team down here on the double."

"Yes, Captain." Spock turned to leave. As he did so McCoy moved to get out of his way. Those few steps were

all that was necessary to bring him within reach of the
Vendorian.

Powerful tentacles snapped out and enveloped the doctor in a constricting grasp.

"Jim!"

Kirk and Spock moved as one toward the Vendorian.
Unraveling the clutching limbs, the alien sent McCoy
spinning and stumbling into the other two officers. All
three fell to the floor.

Moving with surprising agility for such an awkard-look-
ing creature, the Vendorian dashed past them. Spock
managed to roll over in time to make a grab at the fleeing
alien. All he got was a handful of something that felt like
snakeskin without the scales. He couldn't hold it. A second later it was out the doorway and long gone.

Kirk was on his feet, racing for the exit. Spock made a
move as if to follow, instead changed direction and went
directly to the wall communicator.

"Spock to bridge—put me on the ship's intercom, Lieutenant." And then, seconds later, "All security teams, intruder alert! All security teams, repeat, intruder alert—"

Kirk was out in the hall. He looked to his right, then
left, just in time to catch a last glimpse of the Vendorian
turning down an intersecting corridor. A security team
raced around the far end of the hallway facing him a second later. Spock's voice sounded loud, replayed over every speaker in the starship.

"Intruder is a Vendorian, capable of assuming any
shape or form of the same approximate mass . . ."

III

A Jeffries tube loomed nearby. The Vendorian, using
its ability to look in all directions at once, satisfied itself
that no pursuer was in sight. Then it clambered into the
tube.

Moving like a big orange spider, it made its way up the channeled interior. Footsteps sounded below—far away now, muffled with increasing distance—as Kirk and the security team raced through the corridor below.

Near the top, the alien paused and crossed upper tentacles. Once more it shifted to the shape of Carter Winston. A few more centimeters, a careful look both ways, and then he scrambled out of the tube onto a new deck, setting the tube cover back into place.

There were drawbacks as well as advantages to assuming human shape. For one thing, he could no longer see in all directions. So he didn't see Anne Nored until he rounded a corner and nearly ran her down. She staggered and, reflexively, it seemed, he caught her to keep her from falling.

But this time, instead of moving into his arms, she pushed away and brought up her security phaser. It centered squarely on his chest.

Affecting an air of mild surprise he looked first at the phaser, then up at her.

"Anne, what are you doing?"

"My job," she replied tightly. "It isn't hard to guess who the intruder is. You're the only stranger aboard, Carter. Or whatever you are. A . . . a Vendorian." Running footsteps sounded from somewhere behind them. She stared at him, then threw a quick, nervous look over her shoulder.

It was only an instant, but Carter Winston's reflexes were faster than human. He knocked the phaser from her hand. It skittered across the deck to bounce off the far wall. She ran to recover it. At the same time Kirk and a small group of security personnel rounded a far curve.

Anne picked up the phaser, turned and dropped to one knee, holding the phaser in both hands and balancing an elbow on her thigh. It was easy to take aim at the distant figure. She had a clear shot.

But she didn't fire. Instead, she slowly lowered the phaser to her side.

The security team pounded past in pursuit. Kirk slowed and stopped beside her.

"Lieutenant Nored, you could have stopped him ... it. Why didn't you fire?"

She spoke slowly as she got to her feet, without looking at him. "I couldn't. I know some explanation is necessary, Captain, but—" She couldn't think of anything to say that would make her sound less of an idiot.

"I knew he had to be the intruder, but ... I couldn't bring myself to fire!" Her voice was trembling.

"He's an alien, Lieutenant—not Carter Winston. A Vendorian. A shape-changing complex of orange tentacles topped by an inhuman brain."

"My mind tells me that, Captain, but there are other parts of me that don't convince so easily." There, she was right. She still sounded like an idiot.

"Lieutenant," and Kirk's voice was surprisingly devoid of reproach, "the man you loved no longer exists. Carter Winston is dead. He's probably been dead for years."

"I realize that, Captain. But I just—" She turned away. Words had become thoroughly inadequate. "Reason and love don't work well together."

"When you're a commander you can be profound, Lieutenant. For now—" He didn't get the chance to finish. Spock arrived, panting slightly.

"Security teams report no sign of the alien on this deck any longer, Captain."

"How do they know, Mr. Spock?" Kirk sighed. "I was afraid of this. Once out of sight, he can turn into anyone or anything on board this ship. I wonder why he chose to re-form as Carter Winston, instead of as Dr. McCoy or myself?"

"I cannot guess, Captain. I can only surmise that this constant shape changing is not as easy for him as it appears to be to us. He really requires a form capable of mobility now—an examination table or section of wall will no longer do, for example. Perhaps changing into a familiar shape is simpler and less tiring. He is obviously well acquainted with the shape of Carter Winston."

"As a matter of fact," Kirk began, then paused, grinning sardonically. Spock watched him patiently.

"You can at least share the idea with me, Captain, if not the actual humor."

"Oh, nothing, Spock. For a minute it occurred to me ... I thought—" and he grinned wider, "I thought that you might be the Vendorian now." Spock did not smile, which was hardly a surprise.

"What makes you think I'm not, Captain?" Both eyebrows moved ceilingward. Kirk stopped chuckling, gave Spock a uncertain glance before grinning again.

"The Vendorian can change his shape, but not certain other things. I think I'll take a chance on your being you, Spock."

"That is most considerate of you, Captain. We find ourselves in complete agreement on who I am. The question remains," and he paused for effect, "are you who you claim to be?"

"I was with Lieutenant Nored while the alien was still present," Kirk claimed indignantly. "It's a definite problem, all right. If we're not careful he'll have us shooting at each other. But given time, we'll find him. It's only one problem."

Somewhere in space exists a formless, malignant entity who listens to the words of starship captains merely for the chance of playing their plans false. Said entity must have been listening to Kirk, for, as if on cue, the red-alert signal now commenced its visual and aural clamoring. A blinker just above them flashed insistently for attention.

Various crew members began to appear, running towards their battle stations. As any well-drilled crew should, they ignored their two senior officers in single-minded pursuit of current objectives—namely, getting to where they belonged as fast as was humanly or inhumanly possible.

"Now what?" Kirk's question was more resigned than hopeful. He moved to the flashing wall communications hookup.

"Hello, bridge? This is the captain speaking. Scotty? What's happening up there? What's the Vendorian up to now?"

"It's not the Vendorian, Captain," the chief engineer replied. "I wish it were. A pair of Romulan battle cruisers, sir, and if they're not on an intercept course we're about to witness the biggest cosmic coincidence since that double star in M-31 went nova together."

"All right, Scotty, keep a lid on things. We'll be right up."

"What was that you just said about dealing with only one problem, Captain?"

"Spock, if I didn't know that you weren't prone to malicious sarcasm, I'd . . . ahhh, never mind."

By the time they'd regained the bridge and Kirk had resumed his seat in the commander's chair and Spock his own at the library computer, the two Romulans were close enough for visual contact via the telescopic eyes of the main viewscreen.

If there were any chance they might have been Federation ships, that hope was soon laid to rest at the sight of their distinctive silhouettes. In design and basic construction they were similar to the battle cruisers of the Klingon Empire. Insignia and certain minor but unmistakable differences branded them as Romulan.

Kirk's first thought was to get something down on record. Not only in case hostilities ensued, but also because such information would be needed for any legal actions that might arise out of this encounter. So he quickly activated the log.

He was about to begin the entry when a sudden thought struck him. No, not yet. It was too early to plan for pessimistic eventualities. He flicked off the official log, switched on the general recorder instead.

"Mr. Scott, any chance of us outrunning them?"

"Not now, sir," worried Scott, shaking his head once. "They were right on top of us, Captain, before our sensors even picked 'em up."

"It was as if they were waiting for us, Captain," Sulu added.

"Ummmm." Now he directed his voice and attention to the pick-up grid. "Due to interference by the Vendorian recently discovered on board in the guise of Carter Winston, the *Enterprise* has been detected by ships of the Romulan Empire while violating the Romulan Neutral Zone. By the terms of our treaty, the units of the Romulan fleet have a legal right to seize the *Enterprise*. To complicate matters, we have as yet been unable to apprehend the Vendorian responsible for this situation."

Given the laws against harming intelligent neutrals Kirk naturally didn't add his attendant thoughts—namely, that if and when they did find the troublemaking shape-changer, he'd take great pleasure in tying its seven body tentacles in knots and then opening them again . . . with a meat cleaver.

But right now he had a more difficult situation to focus his attention on.

"We're being scanned, Captain," came Uhura's voice. "And I'm picking up a communications beam. They're attempting to contact us." She hesitated. "Shall I throw up an interference screen, sir?" Kirk thought quickly.

"No point in trying to stall them, Lieutenant. I've got a hunch this particular bunch won't stall." He smiled grimly. "Let's hear what they've got to say. If there's visual with it, put it on the screen. I'd like to see who I'm dealing with . . . and if my face does them any good, they're welcome to it."

Visual there was.

When his reptilian image finally cleared on the main viewscreen the relaxed attitude of the Romulan commander only confirmed the suspicions taking root in Kirk's mind.

"You appear to have a propensity for trespassing in the neutral zone, Captain Kirk. I've been told it has happened once or twice before."

My, but wasn't he a smug one, Kirk thought. What Kirk said was different, however, smoothly conciliatory. That was the best attitude Kirk could fake; he couldn't quite bring himself to be deferential toward this oily character.

"It was not deliberate, I assure you."

The Romulan commander's reply was dry. "It never is. But the terms of the treaty are clear. They make no provisions for good intentions. I'd like to indulge in the sentiment your people are so fond of and ignore the treaty this time, but, of course, any attempt to contravene the articles, even for friendship's sake, could mean war."

"Surrender your ship, Captain. You will be well

treated. We will release you and your crew at the nearest Federation outpost bordering the neutral zone."

Kirk thought furiously, considering. "I have your personal word of honor on that, Commander? . . ."

"Larus—Commander Larus. I swear by my family and my command, Captain. You and your personnel need have no worries." He tried hard not to gloat. "I have no personal quarrel with you. I must take your ship only to comply with the terms of the treaty between our two governments. I take no personal pleasure in this distasteful deed whatsoever."

I'll just bet you don't, you grinning reptilian so and so, Kirk silently cursed. His return smile, however, was equally pleasant.

"I'd like a few minutes to inform my crew. There will be certain preparations required."

"Of course, Captain Kirk. I understand perfectly. The shock, and all. Take all the time you need—up to five minutes your ship-time, no more." Abruptly, the screen blanked.

"Transmission ended, Captain," Uhura informed him. "But they're still scanning us."

"Fine. Let 'em scan us till their scanning computers get an electronic migraine." Kirk turned and activated a switch on the right armrest. Spock left his station and moved to stand next to the captain.

"Kirk to security. What's the status on the search for the Vendorian?"

"Nored here, sir." The voice of the lieutenant was calm and professional now, no sign of emotional upset. Good. "No progress yet. We have all decks under constant patrol. No one has seen it, but—"

"How do you know, Lieutenant?" snapped a frustrated Kirk. "Anyone might have walked right past the Vendorian a dozen times without seeing it."

"I don't think so, Captain." Nored's response was firm, confident. "Our patrols have their phasers set on low-power stun. I've given orders that they're to randomly beam everything they pass—walls, ceilings, fixtures—without design or selectivity. We'll end up with a lot of scorched paint, but I think the Vendorian will think twice before he considers staying in one disguise very long."

"And the patrols are traveling in tight groups, guarding one another. So I don't think there's much chance of him turning into one of our own people. At least the alien will be too busy changing shapes to cause any more trouble."

Kirk found himself in agreement with Nored's precautions. It ought to flush the alien out in the open. "Carry on, Lieutenant." He broke the connection and nodded toward the viewscreen where the Romulan ships were displayed again.

"As Scotty points out, Mr. Spock, this meeting is hardly a coincidence. The Romulans were expecting us from the first. The wreck of Winston's ship—I wonder what *did* happen to him—was used to slip a saboteur and spy on board. And what better spy than a shape-changing Vendorian who can become at will any of the spied-upon?

"When I went to my cabin he put me out long enough to take my shape. Then *he* came to the bridge and ordered the course change. By the time I recovered, well," he shrugged, "it was too late to swing free of the zone. A neat trap."

"It would seem so, Captain. Yet one thing continues to puzzle me."

"Spock?"

"How is it that the Romulans are able to persuade a Vendorian to work for them? I cannot think of a logical reason why one of the shape-changers should. I cannot imagine what inducement the Romulans could offer."

"We'll consider the question of motivation later, Mr. Spock. Right now we've got a starship to save." He looked to the helm. "Open a hailing frequency, Lt. M'ress. Uhura, you keep listening for more of the same from our friends out there. And keep monitoring their scans."

The feline navigation officer moved to obey, her tail flicking in nervous response. "I have contact, Captain," she purred. "Hailing frrequency was harrdly necessarry. They've been waiting forr us to rrespond, it seems."

Once again the view of the paired Romulan cruisers was replaced by a portrait of their commander. He was making a strong attempt, Kirk noted, to suppress his normal arrogance.

"Your time is up, Captain. I assume you are now prepared to turn your ship over to me."

"Wrong assumption, Commander."

"Captain," protested the Romulan indignantly, "you are outnumbered, outgunned, and legally in the wrong. I admire your courage, but permit me to say that you err in your tactical evaluation of the present situation."

"I have no choice, Commander," Kirk shot back. "If I were an innocent violator of neutral space that would lead to some discussion, yes. But the treaty also states that deception of any kind—false beacons, signals, anything—used to lure a vessel into the neutral zone are a provocation by the luring side and not by the intruder. It is you who are in violation of the treaty, not I."

"Lured, Captain?" protested the Romulan with admirable outrage. "How could we possibly *lure* a starfleet vessel so deeply into the neutral zone?"

"Through the use of a spy masquerading as a dead human named Carter Winston."

The Romulan commander paused to perform his race's equivalent of a sad shake of the head. "A shape-changing spy? Come now, Captain," he pleaded. "Your courage, it seems, is exceeded only by your imagination. Both are misdirected."

"You used a Vendorian," Kirk continued easily, "which, I might add, is also in violation of a number of treaties, not to mention a violation of the galactic quarantine of Vendoria itself."

Either the Romulan commander decided to abandon his bluff, or else all this forced camaraderie was getting on his nerves. His natural brusqueness abruptly came to the fore.

"Your five minutes are long since up, Captain. Either surrender your ship or prepare to fight."

"I will not surrender my ship," Kirk replied, spacing the words deliberately.

So they were going to fight, mused Chief Engineer Scott.

He had left the bridge after the red-alert signal and

gone to his battle station back in engineering. Well, they'd had trouble with the Romulans before and had come out okay. Even though they were outnumbered this time, he wasn't especially worried. Why, they'd give—

He paused at the top of the spiral ladder. Just in front of him, away from the ladder exit, a crewman was working in front of an open panel. The panel shouldn't have been open. And no one, but no one, should have been working at those relays without Scott's personal permission.

"Hey! What d'you think you're doin'?" The crewman turned quickly.

"Why, nothing, Chief." He walked over to the ladder exit and helped Scott up the last step. "Only this."

He touched Scott's shoulder with a hand. Moving rapidly, he managed to catch the slumping form of the chief engineer before it could slide back down the ladder. Pulling him gently out of the spiral he laid the limp body out on the deck. The crewman rose, again studying the open panel.

Someone else might come and he was in a hurry. Might as well revert to self. The extra limbs would make the job go faster. He crossed his arms, and blurred.

Using only a pair of tentacles for support, the Vendorian used the other five to tear at the thick cables running behind the open panel . . .

The first red light appeared on Sulu's console.

"Captain," he shouted as he worked frantically at the controls beneath the warning flash, "our deflector shields are coming down!"

Kirk cursed silently, pressed a switch on the chair. "Kirk to engineering. Bridge to engineering! Scotty, what's happening back there? Our shields are fading!"

In the main engineering room a tall subengineer rushed to the chattering intercom and acknowledged the call breathlessly.

"H . . . here, sir."

"Not very well you don't. Who is this?" Kirk demanded. "Who's talking?"

"Second Engineer Gabler, sir . . . Captain." Kirk

glanced back at Spock. This was no time for disciplinary action. "Get those shields up again, Gabler—now!"

"I can't, sir!" yelled the other helplessly.

"Well then, rouse Mr. Scott from his nap and have him do it!" Now the response from the other end was one of complete confusion.

"I was just going to ask to speak to him, sir. Isn't he up forward with you?"

"No, he is not up forward with me, Mister. You know the chief's battle station is back there."

"Yes, sir. But he isn't anywhere around, sir."

"Well, then—!" Kirk paused and counted to six, spoke more quietly. "All right, Mr. Gabler. It is vital that we have our shields back as soon as possible. Do the best you can."

"Aye, sir." Gabler switched off, looked around at the small cluster of engineers and technicians who'd gathered around the intercom station.

"Don't just stand there gaping like idiots! The deflector shields have dropped. Check your telltales, trace the leads, find the trouble spot!"

Immediately the group hurried to their positions. Gabler ran to his, too, but his mind wasn't on the technical problem at hand.

What had happened to the chief?

Meanwhile a telltale of a different kind was flashing on Sulu's console. "Shuttle-bay doors are functioning, sir. The Vendorian must be trying to escape."

"We still have some control over this ship," Kirk muttered through clenched teeth. "Shut those doors, and lock all entrances to the shuttle bay."

Sulu tried one switch, frowned.

"No response, sir."

"Emergency override, Mr. Sulu," came Spock's quiet voice. "Mechanism voluntary jam to prevent air loss." He glanced at Kirk as Sulu hurried to obey. "We will not be able to operate the shuttle doors until the stripped relays and gears are replaced, Captain."

Kirk hardly heard him. The same idea had occurred to him seconds after Spock had given the order.

"Doors closing, sir!" reported Sulu excitedly. That was the signal for Kirk to jump from his chair.

"One problem down. Spock, take command. Talk to the Romulans. Stall them. Tell them anything. Tell them we're going to agree, but that I'm desperately thinking of a way to save face—their commander should understand that.

"Uhura, send a security team to the shuttle deck, but don't open the doors yet. We've got the Vendorian trapped, that's enough for now. I'll be back in engineering. I've got to find out what the devil's happening back there."

As he hurried rapidly toward the heart of the starship, Kirk pondered their chances. The shields hadn't fallen all the way, but the *Enterprise*'s defenses had been badly weakened. Even with all shields up and operating at full strength, the *Enterprise* versus two Romulan battle cruisers wasn't exactly a mop-up operation.

Now, with their shield strength down at least fifty percent, well—

At least, he mused with savage satisfaction, they'd prevented the escape of the Vendorian spy. Spock's query came back to him. He, too, wondered how the Romulans had managed to convince the shape-changer to do the dirty work for them. From what little he knew of Vendorian civilization, the alliance made no sense.

After what seemed like hours, he finally reached the main engineering bay. In response to his questions, a harried technician directed him up to another deck. A short climb and he emerged in the middle of another, larger group of milling crew members. One directed him forward. He found Gabler and Scott hunched over an open panel.

"What happened, Scotty?"

"Hello, sir. I'm sure I don't know. I came up here to battle-check the backup deflector-shield relays." His voice took on a tone of puzzled outrage. "And here was this common tech, calm as you please, taking the connections to pieces!"

"Now, the sight of me in such a situation ought to have frozen the good man solid to the deck—workin' unauthorized with such equipment. Instead, he just smiled confident as you please and came over to help me on deck. That's all I remember."

"He couldn't have been at it long, sir," put in Gabler. "We found the chief right after I talked to you."

"He was at it long enough," growled Scotty. The chief's attitude did not inspire feelings of confidence in Kirk.

"How long will it take to fix, Scotty?"

"At least two hours, Captain."

Two *hours!*

"Well, get on it. That's all." Kirk turned and left. He knew better than to make melodramatic pronouncements. If Scott said it would take two hours, it would do no good for Kirk to say, "Do it in one!" The chief engineer's time estimates were as reliable as his work. Two hours then, working at top speed, and he'd have his shields back.

But could they possibly stall the Romulans for two hours, when the Romulan commander had given him five minutes, and those reluctantly? They might not have two seconds left.

They had one bargaining chip left, just one—and that was the *Enterprise* herself.

Already the Romulan commander had admitted that his only interest was in the starship—intact and in working order. If the Romulan's sensors were worth a handful of component's, they'd know by now that the *Enterprise's* shields had been severely weakened. Kirk didn't think they'd hold off forcing a decision in order to give their Vendorian a chance to escape. If he got away, all well and good . . . a bonus. If not, he had served his purpose.

However, they *would* hesitate before destroying the prize they'd worked so hard to snare. How long the vision of the *Enterprise* as a captured ship would keep the Romulan commander's natural belligerence in check Kirk didn't know, and that was the crucial factor.

A destroyed *Enterprise* would be a small blow to Federation strength compared to a fully operational captured one—but a blow nonetheless.

Kirk had no choice. He'd have to take the chance the Romulans wanted the starship badly enough to hold off firing on her. Nerves and not phasers would decide the outcome of this confrontation.

He smiled and felt a little better.

There were worse things to bet on than the avarice of a Romulan. . . .

IV

A single shuttle craft was lined up facing the *Enterprise*'s bay doors. Those doors wouldn't open now until a number of highly trained people had replaced certain stripped bearings and other deliberately ruined parts.

Three security guards had actually made it into the bay before the order to lock all doorways had taken effect. One of them was lying slumped across the open portway leading into the shuttle. Another lay crumpled at the foot of the ramp leading up into it.

The third stood quietly facing the other occupant of the soundless chamber.

Anne Nored kept her phaser pointed at him. The hand holding it didn't waver, didn't shake. Neither did her voice.

"You're not getting past me this time. I've learned my lesson."

The form of Carter Winston nodded slowly. "Yes, he said you were like this. Efficient, professional, as well as affectionate and beautiful. You're quite everything he said you were, Anne." The muzzle of the powerful phaser didn't dip a centimeter.

There was suspicion in her gaze, hesitancy in her voice—but she had to ask.

"Carter . . . what did he say? How . . . how do you know him so well?"

The Winston/Vendorian spoke. Despite the fact that instinct told her she should regard its every word as a

clever lie, there was something in Winston's voice that ...
no, darn it, not Winston's! Only a sly mimicry, an
uncanny imitation.

Reproduction or not, something in the voice sounded
almost honest.

"He said many things. Some were feelings, deep feelings he could not always fully express or adequately convey. Emotions that, while I understood the words and the
flat meanings of them, clearly held a good deal more than
I could comprehend. Language can sometimes be infuriat-
ingly uncommunicative, can tease and confuse instead of
enlighten.

"I tried hard to understand these feelings. So many of
the ideas and concepts that he tried to convey to me were
new, alien, strange—but always intriguing. The less I understood, the more I wanted to know." Winston shook his
head.

"My people have their faults, but they are compounded
by this peculiar ability of ours to mimic others, to change
our shape. Something so natural to us seems so frighten-
ingly strange to other intelligent beings. I understand that
lower creatures on many worlds can perform similar feats.
But when the ability is coupled with intelligence, other
races grow nervous.

"Sometimes," he continued bitterly, "we—" His voice
shifted back to a more gentle tone. "But Carter Winston
truly loved you."

The phaser shifted ever so slightly, but still remained
fixed on the figure in front of her. Blazes, where were the
backup security personnel?

She had no way of knowing that Kirk had ordered the
shuttle bay sealed off from the rest of the ship. Where was
the captain, or Mr. Spock? Someone to give orders, to
take this responsibility off her hands.

She ought to have said nothing to the creature, ought to
have kept her mouth shut, and at least beamed it slightly
in one leg to restrict its movement.

Instead, she asked softly, "How did he die?"

"Winston's ship did indeed encounter severe meteor activity in open space. But the damage it sustained was not
from the swarm Captain Kirk found me drifting in. The

deflector shields of his small ship were too weak to protect him from the violent assault of that original storm.

"The shields held only long enough for him to locate a possible landing site and refuge. The only one—Vendoria. Winston knew that world was under edict, forbidden to travelers, but he had no choice in the matter. It was a miracle he managed to land his vessel at all. Neither he nor his ship, however, survived the landing intact. His injuries were severe." Winston shuffled his feet.

"As is our custom, upon conclusion of primary surgery he was left in the care of a single one of us." He looked straight at her. "Me. He lived on for almost four of your years before the damage to his system exceeded the repair capabilities of our medical science."

"We became very close in those four years." There was a pause while the two looked at each other—one perhaps a little too human, the other a great deal less so.

Or was he?

"You're so much like him—his voice, his little gestures, his mannerisms. Even the inflections in certain words."

"You must understand, Anne, that my people enjoy our talent for mimicry. It is pleasure to us. But because of it we are cut off from the rest of the civilized galaxy. Therefore anything new to imitate is regarded as a great novelty. To a large extent it becomes the exclusive property of its discoverer. So it was with myself and Carter Winston.

"I often went about in his shape, this shape. For longer and longer periods of time. A most remarkable form. Wearing it gave me the greatest pleasure, because it fit so well not only physically but mentally.

"And I think Winston himself enjoyed seeing me in his own image. While my own form was not repulsive to him—as an interstellar trader he had no primitive shape prejudices—I think the chance to see and to speak with ... himself ... made it easier for him in his last days." Winston smiled.

"It was not as though he died with only an alien monster at his side."

"And he did say that he loved me?"

"Yes. Often. And that brings up another problem." He hesitated. "You see, I feel I absorbed a great many of the attitudes and emotions he felt. The longer I was with him, the more strongly ingrained these attitudes became. I do not know how it is with humans, but a Vendorian cannot remain in close association, let alone in the same shape, of another being without becoming in a sense a part of him."

"There were times, after our association had grown close, that when Winston grew hungry, I was hungry. If he felt tired and exhausted, I grew tired and exhausted. It became deeper than that. If he felt pain then I, in his form, was hurt. We would commiserate together on his sad situation. I would cheer him and he would attempt to raise my spirits."

"Our unity grew even to the point where when he would feel homesick, I could feel a deep longing for a world I had never seen, would never set foot on. And," his voice dropped lower, "his love for you was very, very strong. I could not help but be affected by such a strong emotion." He looked up at her again.

"Because I was there when he died, Anne, it did not end."

Unwillingly, she found herself shaking. She let the phaser drop low, lower. He could have made a move toward her at any time now, but he didn't. All thoughts of aggression had vanished from her mind. A suspicious moisture began to form at the corners of her eyes. She raised a free hand, tried to brush it away. It wasn't possible. Tears started to trickle down her cheeks in most unmilitary fashion.

Both hands came up, but this time it was to reach out to him, instinctively.

"Carter—"

He moved close. One hand touched the fingers gripping the phaser. She didn't resist. His hands moved high, held her firmly by the shoulders and pushed gently away.

"You must not weep for me."

"Carter, I—"

"Anne, this is what I am."

He stepped back and crossed both arms over his chest. Carter Winston disappeared.

In his place rose a tall, seven-tentacled entity, a nightmare shape of thick orange cables and a bulbous, bejeweled head. It spoke, and the voice was the voice of Carter Winston—but now sounding oddly distant, echoing. It came from a voicebox no longer human.

"How could you love . . . this?"

Her hands dropped from her mouth, to which they'd jerked with the first gasp of surprise. Like most humans, she'd never seen a Vendorian. The form was as inhuman and thoroughly alien as the wildest dreams of drug-induced narcosis.

But the first shock passed. The creature crossed tentacles and once again shifted into the familiar figure of Carter Winston. There was sympathy in its once-again human voice and . . . something else?

"You see why I told you it would be best to forget me," the alien said, unaware of the change in pronoun.

"But unfortunately, *I* can't," came the voice of Captain Kirk. Both figures turned to face a side entrance. Kirk had arrived moments ahead of the requested security team. He held a phaser on Winston.

He never had a chance to use it, because the shock wave from the first bolt fired by the Romulan phaser banks threw them all to the floor of the hanger. Dazed, Kirk rolled over, tried to force himself to his feet and focus the phaser at the same time. His vision cleared rapidly and he glanced around the shuttle bay, looking frantically in all directions.

As expected, the alien was gone again.

He noticed Anne Nored. She had one hand on her forehead and was having difficulty getting to her feet. Kirk helped her up.

"Carter . . . Carter . . ."

"The Vendorian is gone, Lieutenant Nored," said Kirk tightly. "I've got to get back to the bridge. Will you be all right?"

"Yes, just a bump. I've got to get back to security." She took a step and almost fell over.

Kirk half carried, half guided her to the exit. The security team met them there.

"Ensign Tuan reporting, Captain." The excited junior officer was trying to look at Kirk respectfully and over his shoulder into the cavernous shuttle bay at the same time. "Where's the alien, sir?"

"The alien is gone again, Mr. Tuan. And stop waving that phaser around before you hurt yourself." The ensign looked properly abashed and hurried to holster the weapon. Kirk sighed.

"Post a guard here. The outer doors are jammed, but the alien might try to burn an exit for the shuttle. Alert the armory and engineering. And security central. They'll have to start the search over again, but maybe we can keep the thing confined to this deck, this time."

"Yes, sir."

"Lieutenant Nored, somehow I think security can manage without you." She didn't look up at him. "You come to the bridge with me. There's a chance you might be useful there."

He felt like adding a few other choice comments. She'd had the alien trapped again and once more it had escaped. While he found himself sympathizing with her state of mind, he couldn't condone her actions. Mr. Spock would be even less understanding. Meanwhile, it would be better for her on the bridge, away from the actual search. It was a better alternative than the brig.

Besides, it would be hard to claim she had let the thing get away voluntarily. The Romulans had contributed to that.

Yes, what about the Romulans?

Spock was waiting with a report. He started talking before Kirk had resumed his seat. Anne Nored wandered around the bridge, looking lost. She was still numbed, and not entirely from being thrown to the deck.

"Direct hit, Captain," Spock informed him calmly. "There is some damage to the secondary propulsive systems. Their commander has apparently weighed his choices and has concluded we've had enough time to make up our minds. He's ready to fight."

"I only felt one shock wave, Mr. Spock. No subsequent attacks?"

"No, Captain. Only the single phaser strike."

"Then he's hoping to force our hand, one way or the other, but he still wants the ship. There's nothing in the damaged section but automatic machinery. He's trying to avoid casualties at this point, trying to disable us without giving a reason for an all-out battle."

He looked back to Lt. M'ress, at the communications console now, as she broke in on his summary.

"The Rromulan commanderr is signaling, sirr. Shall I put him on the scrreen?"

"I'd rather you put him . . . go ahead, Lieutenant."

A moment later the face of the Romulan leader had once more taken the place of his ships on the main viewscreen.

The Romulans would make terrible poker players, Kirk reflected. Their expressions were even broader and less inhibited than those of humans. Their ambassadors and consuls must have a terrible time practicing the wiles of diplomacy.

For example, the commander now undoubtedly thought he was maintaining the Romulan equivalent of a straight face, but his expectant smile reached from ear to ear.

"Captain Kirk," he began, and there was unconcealed anticipation in his voice, too. I wonder what he's up to now, Kirk mused. He didn't relish the pickle they'd gotten themselves into.

"All our main batteries are trained on your ship. I have observed a . . . ah, singular lack of defensive effort on your part. To resist at this point would be not only useless but criminally wasteful of life.

"If you have no regard for yourself or your ship, think of your crew. Our recent attack was intentionally directed at uninhabited areas of your ship. I cannot guarantee the selectivity of gunners in the future." He managed to look apologetic as he leaned forward slightly.

"Will you now surrender your vessel? As you know, my people are not in the habit of giving second chances."

That was the Romulan's way of telling him that, yes, he wanted the *Enterprise* and no, he didn't want it enough to give him any more time. Kirk's thoughts raced.

He might be able to figure a way out of this, if the back of his mind wasn't busy worrying about what the Vendorian was up to. And he could cope with the Vendorian if it wasn't for the Romulans. But the two of them together!

It didn't matter. He didn't have any more time, anyway.

Without full deflectors, he thought angrily, we're just a clay pigeon for them. Kirk had never seen a clay pigeon in his life and probably wouldn't have recognized one if it had fallen into his lunch. But archaic metaphors had a way of sticking around in the terran language.

"Practicality does suggest capitulation at this point, Captain," observed Spock. "I, too, see no solution to our present dilemma. There are other starships, there is no other self."

Of course, there are other ships, Kirk thought. But how much chance would he have of getting another command after giving up the *Enterprise* without firing a shot?

And what chance did his crew have? Could he guarantee their safety once the *Enterprise* was in Romulan hands?

Sulu had been morosely monitoring inship as well as exterior sensors, checking his gauges and dials. Now he interrupted Spock's advice excitedly ... interrupted Kirk's depression. Interrupted all action on the bridge.

"Captain, I don't understand ... but the deflector shields are coming up again!"

In two steps Kirk was at his shoulder, staring down at the indicators in disbelief. "It's only one shield—"

"Yes, sir, but it's our prime defensive screen, and it's between us and the Romulans. Look," he pointed to one energy gauge, "it's operating at full strength."

Kirk rushed back to his chair. A wise man does not question the sudden appearance of a cache of spears when the barbarians are at his gate. He throws them. Time to question their origin when pulling them *out* of his attackers.

They had to act immediately, before some idle technician on one of the battle cruisers noticed the resurgence of strength in the *Enterprise*'s defensive fields.

"Mr. Sulu, aim for the propulsion units on the lead Romulan vessel. Phasers and photon torpedoes in combination." Sulu's hands played the controls like an organ.

"Phasers and torpedoes ready, sir."

"We've got to get one with this first burst, Mr. Sulu."

"Will do, Captain."

"Fire!"

"Firing, sir."

"Evasive action. Mr. Sulu, keep that good screen between us and the Romulans."

The Romulan commander had long since vanished from the screen. M'ress had automatically substituted the sensor view of the two battle cruisers. It was too bad, in a way. Kirk would have given a lot to see the commander's face right now.

He could see the phaser beams striking at the rear of the nearest ship.

"They're pursuing, sir," reported Sulu evenly. "Both of them."

Kirk only nodded. They'd probably expected him to try and run, but not to fight.

There was a sudden bright flash at the stern of the first ship. The Romulan's screens had handled the *Enterprise*'s heavy phasers, but one, possibly two, of the powerful photon torpedoes had slipped through their screens. The wounded vessel seemed to hesitate, then vanished instantly from the screen—not destroyed, but slowed.

"Second vessel firing Captain," said Spock. Kirk tensed.

"Phasers and—" Before he could finish, the bridge rocked to a strong shock wave as the *Enterprise* took the force of the attack from the remaining pursuer. This was no disabling strike, but one designed to tear the starship apart.

The amazingly resurgent deflector shield held. Artificial gravity stabilized and the regular ship's lights remained on.

"Minor damage to E and H decks," reported Spock moments later. "Casualties on E deck, minor hulling and air loss in four compartments. Automatic sealant is handling the damage."

"Lock on second target," Kirk ordered calmly. He noticed M'ress looking at him with admiration. She didn't sweat, but she was panting heavily—nervous, Kirk knew. Obviously she didn't know that starship captains only sweated on the inside of their skins. That's why they were so irritable all the time.

"Locking on second vessel, Captain," came Sulu's reply. A second later, "locked on, sir."

"Phasers and torpedoes, Mr. Sulu. Stagger the torps, try to run them at the same spot." Maybe they could overload the Romulan's shields at one point. Discouraging her ought to be as effective as destroying her.

"Firing, Captain."

There were brilliant flashes on the screen from the vicinity of the Romulan ship as her screens reeled under the dual assault. Sulu's eyes remained glued to his indicators, his voice a battle monotone.

"Phasers . . . direct hit, sir." There was a flash so bright it blanked out the screen for a moment. "Two photon torpedo hits."

But the Romulan, now warned, had brought his shields up to maximum power and had taken the blinding energies without damage. Kirk heard Spock's report and tried not to look disappointed. If the Romulan computers got a torpedo in behind their one good deflector shield . . .

"Prepare to fire again, Mr. Sulu."

"Standing by, sir."

The third attack wasn't necessary. One second the Romulan ship was hard in pursuit, the next it was fading rapidly from sensor range as her commander broke off the engagement and headed back into the depths of the neutral zone.

"Losing contact, sir," reported Sulu. "She's arcing."

Kirk's voice was full of relief and satisfaction. "Going back to help her disabled companion. Good. A fight to the end wouldn't do either side any good."

"Maybe the pounding we gave the first one," Sulu began, but Kirk was shaking his head.

"I don't think so, Mr. Sulu. The Romulans exhibit a number of reprehensible characteristics, but cowardice isn't one of them. No, they were expecting our defenses to collapse. That's why they didn't attack right away. When our shields suddenly went back up—

"Their whole plan from the moment of interception was predicated on a number of things happening. When their carefully laid schedule started to go awry, they decided to call it off. The Romulans like their ambushes neatly planned in advance. They don't like surprises.

"Speaking of surprises, Mr. Spock, exactly how badly did we damage that other Romulan? Check your recorders, please." Spock turned back to the library computer console, activated the request.

"I hope it wasn't too bad," Kirk added. "Severe damage or loss of life might force the Romulan High Command into continuing a fight they've lost interest in. They've got a lot of pride." Spock's answer relieved Kirk's concern on that score.

"First vessel's main power supply was knocked out, Captain. Injuries to personnel should be minimal. She should be able to run on secondary drive, but slowly. With the aid of the other ship the Romulans should be able to repair her well enough to reach their nearest naval station."

Kirk grunted in satisfaction. He swung to look at the elevator as engineer Scott appeared, approaching him.

"Good work, Mr. Scott. That deflector shield went up just in time."

Scott's reaction was not what Kirk expected. Instead of a smile of pleasure at the compliment, the chief engineer looked confused, startled.

"But, sir, the shield connections haven't all been repaired yet. I came forward to see if I could be of help up here. My technicians are still carrying out the final repairs. They'll need over an hour yet, just like I said."

Spock left his library station and walked over to join the conversation.

"Interesting."

"But, confound it, Scotty, the shields went up! At least, the main one did. If you haven't finished repairs, then what—" He paused. A sudden gleam of comprehension dawned.

"Of course! Winston, or rather, the Vendorian."

"It is not outside the realm of possibility, Captain," agreed Spock. "If he could rearrange his own internal structure to become an examination table, one must assume that he could also rearrange himself to become—"

"A deflector shield?" Despite the evidence that seemed to point to the Vendorian, Kirk was doubtful. "And take the uncontrolled energy of a battle cruiser's full assault phasers?" He shook his head. He wanted to believe such a thing was possible, but—

"Vendorians are marvelous mimics, Mr. Spock, but super-beings they're not. No living organism could spread its substance that thin and take that kind of—"

"He did not become the deflector *shield*, Captain," Spock corrected. "There are many instruments—complex controls, switching elements and other electronic components—in a medical examination table. I cannot conceive of a single creature becoming a deflector shield, either, but a series of broken cables, force-links, and other damaged connections? Do not forget, the Vendorian had an excellent look at the very linkages he broke."

Scott had been listening to all this and had achieved nothing except some practice in feeling twitchy. Now his curiosity turned to frustration.

"Will someone please tell me what's been goin' on?" he pleaded, thoroughly confused.

Before either officer could reply, the doors to the elevator dilated again. They all glanced automatically in that direction.

The orange shape that half-stood, half-floated in the portal was by now familiar to Kirk and Spock, but the nightmarish image was something new to Scott and the other bridge personnel. M'ress hissed softly.

"What manner of beastie is that?" gulped Scott.

"That is your deflector shield, Mr. Scott," said Spock.

"My defle—" Scott's look showed he wasn't sure which was more alien—the thing in the doorway or the ship's first officer. He looked back at the Vendorian.

"That is essentially true," the Vendorian commented in the voice of Carter Winston. It sidled toward them. "I did what I could." Despite its multiple lenses, it turned and seemed to face Kirk, a human gesture.

"I assume the danger to your ship is over, Captain?"

"It is. Unless the Romulans have some other surprises."

"I do not believe that they do," the Vendorian replied.

"I am glad. I'm sorry that I endangered your ship and your people. Such was not my intention."

Now maybe Kirk could get the answer to a question that had been bothering him ever since they found out that the strange spy was a Vendorian.

"Why did you do it? What possible reward could the Romulans have offered you?"

"To understand that, Captain, it is necessary to tell you a little about myself. The remainder can be supplied by Lieutenant Nored." Kirk glanced over at the lieutenant, who was watching the Vendorian closely.

"My ... attachment ... to the human Carter Winston provoked much comment among my people, Captain. I have always felt and acted somewhat differently from the Vendorian norm. Mental deviates are not treated with compassion on Vendoria.

"As Carter Winston continued to live and I continued to spend more and more time attending him, my aberration became much commented upon. But there was a lock, a bond between us that transcended mere shape and species. I felt I somehow had more in common with the injured human than with other Vendorians.

"They began to shun me. I became an outcast among my own kind, Captain. But this I did not mind ... as long as Winston lived. But when he died, my people continued to look upon me with distaste, to avoid my company and presence. I grew by turns lonely, then bitter, and then desperately lonely once again.

"Though time passed, my situation did not change. I was still treated as a pariah. When a Romulan ship visited the town on whose outskirts I lived as a recluse—" He paused. "They have been visiting Vendoria quite regularly, by the way, for the past several of your years, always hoping to ally themselves with my people. But we would have none of them."

"Interesting," commented Spock. "I must make a note of that. I know my father, as well as a number of other ambassadors, will be interested in such information. I expect they will have a few words to exchange with their Romulan counterpart." He moved away, back to the li-

brary station, to dictate a report of the Romulan's violation of the Vendorian quarantine.

"You were saying," prodded Kirk, "that your people
would have nothing to do with the Romulans."

"And why should they? The Romulans had nothing to
offer them. But I," and the faint light of the eye lenses
seemed to glow a little more intensely, "I was another
story. My people had rejected me. I was a useless
outcast."

"The Romulans had nothing to offer me—except a life,
Captain. A chance to perform functions of value. We may
seem at times a frivolous and idle race, but it is literally a
matter of life and death for a Vendorian to be occupied in
a useful function, to be doing something of value.

"Vendoria no longer offered me this; indeed, by their
lack of companionship my people effectively forbade it to
me. So in desperation I agreed to do what the Romulans
requested of me. You must understand, Captain, that
function among us, to be considered worthwhile, must be
of value not only to the doer, but also to someone else."

From the first, Kirk's feelings toward this alien intruder
had been somewhat less than fraternal. But as Winston's
"voice" spun a tale of a tortured past, he found himself
coming to regard the Vendorian less and less as a belligerent invader and more as an individual, a victim of circumstances beyond his control—a prisoner condemned by his
own compassion.

"What finally changed your mind about the Romulans—and us?"

"It seems, Captain, that I have become more Carter
Winston than I knew. Perhaps my friends and associates
on Vendoria sensed it even better than I. My refusal to
recognize this change in myself no doubt drove them even
farther from me.

"I had to fight myself to comply with the Romulans
when they first revealed to me their plan to take your
ship. But finally I realized that if they could not capture
the ship, they were willing to destroy it and all of you on
board. That's when I felt the sorrow that I know Carter
Winston would have felt.

"He loved life and other lives so much, Captain Kirk.

Because of him I could not allow the Romulans to harm Anne, or any of you.

"So as you and Mr. Spock have surmised, I changed myself yet again. I became the very linkages in the deflector system that I had broken. It was ... very difficult. The most difficult change I have ever had to make. The internal arrangements especially had to be so precise, so delicately aligned. I had to structure myself to permit current to pass through my body." He seemed to sway back and forth on those thick tentacles.

"But I could not allow you to come to physical harm through my actions. Through the actions of ... of Carter Winston."

Kirk nodded slowly. "I think I understand. At least, I think I understand as well as it's possible for a non-Vendorian to."

"I cannot go back to the Romulans now," echoed the hollow voice. "I have menaced your ship and its people, and I cannot go back to Vendoria. What will happen to me now?"

This was ridiculous! The creature swaying slowly in front of Kirk had nearly caused the destruction of the *Enterprise*. Kirk had no business, no business at all, feeling sorry for it.

However . . .

"You'll have to stand some sort of trial first, I suppose," Kirk guessed. Abruptly he found himself working very hard and not too successfully to suppress a smile.

"To my knowledge, no Vendorian has ever been tried in a Federation court before. I expect they'll have to make some rather novel arrangements to prevent you from becoming, say, the judge or the jury computer.

"But you did save the *Enterprise* from the Romulans. You've done both good and evil to us in a very short space of time, Vendorian."

"Carter Winston will serve as well as any name, Captain. He has not had need of it for many months, now. And somehow the name feels . . . right."

"Okay, Winston. It will be up to the court to decide whether or not saving us from the very difficulty you plunged us into in the first place obviates your initial belligerence." He touched the back of his neck, remembering.

"Personally, I don't intend to press charges. And I don't think anyone else will, either. It's the gentlest assault I've ever been subjected to."

"Thank you, Captain."

"Until we can put you planetside, I think it would be best for the mental stability of my crew if you remained in the guise of Carter Winston."

"I understand, James Kirk." Tentacles lifted and crossed. Lt. M'ress hadn't witnessed the transformation yet, and she hissed softly. Once more the orange cephalopod was gone, Carter Winston stood in its place.

"I'm also afraid," Kirk continued, trying to put some bite into his voice, "that I'll have to ask you to remain under guard. I'm beginning to trust you, I think, but—"

"That's all right, Captain," smiled Winston. "You'll feel better knowing I'm under observation, at least until we are back in Federation-controlled territory. Knowing that the pair of pants you put on in the morning really are a pair of pants."

"You've appropriated Winston's sense of humor, too, I see." Kirk's smile grew. "I think you're going to be all right . . . Carter. I'll buzz security. One guard ought to be enough." He edged a hand toward the call button.

"Captain, could you possibly assign me that duty?" Kirk had completely forgotten about Anne Nored. He glanced over at her. In doing so he completely missed the expression of surprise that had come over Carter Winston's face.

"But—" Winston stuttered, "you have seen me. You know what I am."

"I've been a starship officer for some years now, Carter," she whispered. "You see, I've changed a little, too. Since we've been apart I've seen a lot of strange things pinwheeling about this universe, even a few that might shock you. In the final analysis form doesn't seem nearly as important as certain other things."

"As Carter Winston—even as a part of him—I think there's a better life for you than the Romulans or anyone else can offer. Oh, damn!" She actually stamped her foot.

"I don't know how to say it—can we at least talk about that?" Her eyes were imploring.

"I don't . . . know." Kirk saw that Winston was totally confused. This was the last thing he'd ever anticipated. Helplessly he looked to Kirk, who nodded at Anne.

"You have the guard detail, Lieutenant."

She smiled. "Thank you, sir." She gazed back at Carter Winston with a look of . . . Kirk shook his head. Anne Nored was right. The universe was indeed full of beautiful, strange, and unexpected surprises.

They headed for the elevator.

As it happened, McCoy was on his way up in the same cab. He moved to one side and watched as alien and Anne got in. The door closed behind them.

The doctor stood pondering for a moment. Then he crossed to where the *Enterprise*'s three other senior officers were clustered in animated conversation.

"You caught him."

"Acute observation, doctor."

McCoy's mouth twisted. "Ho-ho-ho and a Merry Christmas to you, too, Spock." He looked over at Kirk. "I'm glad to see him under guard, Jim. If he'd turned into a second Spock, it would have been too much to take."

How prophetic are the idle jests of man! There would come a time when McCoy would have occasion, if not the desire, to recall that phrase.

But for now it only provoked an innocent chuckle from Kirk and Scott.

"Perhaps so, doctor," the first officer of the *Enterprise* agreed. "But then, two doctor McCoys might just bring the level of medical efficiency on this ship up to acceptable minimums."

"Careful, Doctor McCoy," warned a grinning Scotty as McCoy, topped again, did a slow burn. "I'm not sure life-support can keep things livable with all the heat you're puttin' out."

"Heat? I'll give you heat . . . !" McCoy began.

PART II

THE
LORELEI
SIGNAL

(Adapted from a script by Margaret Armen)

V

They eventually dropped Carter Winston off-ship in the system of Valeria. It was the nearest world to their exit from the neutral zone that was capable of dealing with the peculiar case of Carter Winston.

Not surprisingly, Anne Nored asked to be transferred to the security detail that would keep an eye—several eyes—on the prisoner both prior to and after the trial.

Not surprisingly, Kirk granted her request. He'd already come to the conclusion that if Carter Winston/Whatever was absolved of wrongdoing in diverting the *Enterprise* into the neutral zone—Kirk had told the Vendorian to plead compulsion—the presence of Anne Nored would be the best thing for him.

It would probably also be the best thing for Anne Nored.

He was mildly concerned that the Romulans might still try to make hay of the *Enterprise*'s incursion into the neutral zone, exhibiting their own damaged ship as evidence of the brutal Federation's unrelenting bellicosity.

As it developed, a number of things conspired to prevent this.

For one, there was the fact that the *Enterprise* had encountered not one but two battle-ready, fully prepared cruisers. They'd badly damaged one and put the other to flight, though the Romulans would doubtlessly insist that the second had broken off the engagement only to go to the assistance of its injured comrade.

Far more influential was Spock's official report, with corroboration by Winston, of continued Romulan visitation to the mutually quarantined world of Vendoria. Politicians handled this awkward situation in the usual way. A number of high-ranking officials quietly got together, shared a few drinks and dirty jokes, and decided to let the whole matter drop.

Meanwhile the *Enterprise* lay over in Valerian orbit to take on supplies for the first part of the new year and to make a few much-needed repairs. McCoy, for example, had a chance to go over his medical instrumentation with the testing facilities of a major ground-based hospital. And Scotty had help in repairing the deflector-shield links that Winston had thoroughly disrupted.

Despite her extensive facilities there were still a number of minor components the *Enterprise* required which the orbiting supply station couldn't provide. But nothing the ship couldn't do without.

To obtain them Kirk would have had to travel a fair number of parsecs to the major naval base at Darius IV. Instead, he chose to spend the rest of the holiday season orbiting somnolent, restful Valeria.

While Valeria was still something of an outpost world, its larger cities offered sufficiently sophisticated fleshpots to satisfy the more cosmopolitan tastes of certain of the *Enterprise*'s crew. And her rural attractions sufficed to assuage the nerves of the less adventurous.

In sum, it was an ideal stopover world.

Kirk spent a week fishing at a magnificiently clear, unpolluted mountain lake—relaxing, hiking, and letting his beard grow. At the end of seven days he found the open spaces oddly confining, the theoretical vastness of the mountain valley closing in until the surrounding peaks induced a sensation bordering on the claustrophobic.

A sure sign vacation time was up.

He returned to the *Enterprise*. Two days later the last member of the crew had been rounded up, brought back on board, and either treated for accumulated cuts and bruises, formally bailed out, or sobered up.

While in space his crew formed a perfectly integrated, smoothly functioning machine. But they were a reservoir of human emotions and resentments. Every so often these needed to be drained to keep his personnel healthy. Depending on your point of view, Valeria was the lucky or unlucky world that served as the requisite sponge.

Once back in free space, Kirk set the *Enterprise* on a course that would bring it 'round in a wide swing to pass close by Rifton, one of the Federation's seven principle Starfleet bases.

Kirk blinked, rolled over, and looked at the clock over his bed: 1730 hours. As good a time as any to make the necessary log entry acknowledging the formal orders they'd picked up from Starfleet branch headquarters.

In a sense, the log entry would be only a duplicate of the same orders, but apparently some analyst somewhere decreed it necessary. He sighed. Formal procedure, red tape, bureaucracy—as Einstein had claimed, one could circle the universe and arrive back at the starting point, which always seemed to be a forty-page report in triplicate.

He thumbed the switch activating the pickup in his desk, set the dial for cross-room reception.

"Stardate 5483.7. The *Enterprise* has been ordered to provide standard escort for a small convoy of ore carriers heading toward Carson's World." He didn't add that he thought it an inexcusable waste of starship time, not to mention a colossal bore. The sentiment wouldn't be appreciated.

If he'd known the alternative future he might have thought it otherwise.

"Said ore carriers are to pick up and then transport to Bethulia III four million metric tons of heavy chromium and other duralloy ores." He paused thoughtfully to consider his next words, began again.

"This shipment of alloy ores is necessary to the development of the burgeoning metals industry on Bethulia III, and to the planned construction next fiscal Starfleet year of two and possibly three new deep-space starships. In view of the Federation-Klingon Treaty of 5260 limiting offensive weaponry in this quadrant of space, it appears—" He frowned before really noting the source of the annoyance.

The small viewscreen set on his desk was blinking

steadily, a demanding yellow glow. Someone had a message for him that couldn't wait. Irritably he shut off the log and swung his legs out of bed. It had *better* be important!

The viewer beeped as he approached the desk, and a green light winked on on the lower left side of the screen. Lt. Uhura was warning him that ready or not, the call was on its way in.

He sat down in front of the screen and activated the knob that would tell Uhura he was indeed present, alive, and well.

"Kirk here. What is it, Lieutenant?"

"Deep-space call from Starfleet Science Center, sir," Uhura's voice explained.

"But we've already received our—" He stopped. Someone on Rifton badly wanted to get in touch with the *Enterprise,* badly enough to requisition power to boost a transmission signal across the rapidly widening distance between them. It occurred to him that anyone who had the authority to do so might be rather an important person—and in a hurry.

He blinked the sleep from his eyes. "Put it through, Lieutenant Uhura."

The blurred image that started to form was confused with the distance and the weakness of the signal, but under Uhura's skillful hands the outside static was rapidly cleared. The picture that finally formed on the screen was that of Vice Admiral for Science Julianna van Leeuwenhook. It was still spotty and streaked with interference, but Kirk knew Uhura was working miracles just to hold it in.

"Captain James Kirk here." The vice admiral smiled slowly, her long gray hair falling in waves to her shoulders. "How are things at Science Center, Admiral? Sorry I missed you."

She shrugged, a slight gesture that might have confessed boredom, might mean something else entirely.

"So am I, Captain. It would have saved me the trouble of this call. But I didn't know until after you'd left contact range that the *Enterprise* was in the area. No need to apologize for skipping a social call. Deep-space transmission is expensive, but ...

"To answer your question, things are the same as usual. Instead of making our work easier, every problem we solve turns up a dozen new ones. Every discovery opens a hundred new avenues of inquiry. While my staff and budget increase arithmetically, the number of projects we are supposed to fulfill—all of them marked top priority, of course—grows geometrically.

"Why, if my people and resources were to quadruple tomorrow, James, in two weeks we'd be hopelessly behind." She smiled.

"Meaning you're not now?" Kirk countered.

"Most certainly we are, Captain. The only difference is, while it's still a hopeless mess, it's an organized hopeless mess." The smile shrank, to be replaced with a no-nonsense frown. "That organization just turned up an interesting discovery. That's what I want to talk to you about. But first, what is your present position and distance from Rifton?"

"Just a second, Admiral." He thumbed the intership comm unit. "Mr. Spock, our present position please?" There was a short pause, then the information came back to him.

"Nine-six-five-five right declension to the galactic plane, a hundred fifty degrees north."

"Thank you, Spock." He repeated the figures for the vice admiral. She nodded and didn't bother to check it on any device. Julianna van Leeuwenhook could do astrogation in her head.

"You've made good time. The ore convoy you're escorting—that was your new assignment, wasn't it?"

"Yes, Admiral," he admitted, steeling himself. The change in tense hadn't gone unnoticed.

"Well, they seem fairly well along their way. You've had no trouble thus far, have you?"

"No, Admiral."

She seemed pleased. "Good. Then I would think they could make it the rest of the way on their own."

"Their captains won't think so."

"They'll have to think so. I'll get in touch with the

commander of the Dervish outpost. He can spare a small ship for the final escort run. He'll have to. The captains of the ore carriers can travel on their own for a while.

"Oh, I know their cargo will be too valuable to consign to a small frigate or some such. But by the time they've finished on-loading at Carson's World I'll have another starship there to meet them." She shifted in her seat, and the incredible communications system instantly transmitted the squeak of chair on floor across the light-years.

"You might even be able to get back to meet them yourself, Captain."

"Get back from where, Admiral?" Obviously their soft, if dull assignment was making off at maximum warp-speed for unexplored regions.

"I'd like the *Enterprise* to make a little detour." She tried to make it sound unimportant, trivial. That really raised the hackles on Kirk's neck.

"It's nothing, really. Shouldn't take you more than a day or two to investigate. The *Enterprise* is the closest ship to the . . . um, affected area."

Kirk sighed. At least it didn't sound like another catastrophe. He still had vivid memories of the Mantilles Incident.

"Yes, Admiral." He hit another switch. "Recording new orders." She leaned forward in her chair.

"You are familiar with the section of peripheral space that is now on—let's see—your port plane? Sector 4423—also known as the Cicada Sector?"

"Cicada?" Kirk's brows drew together as he considered the strange word. Oh, yes, the cicada was a terran insect that spent many years underground to eventually emerge for but a few days of activity in the sunlight before returning to the soil to develop and change.

The name seemed frivolous, too. But was it? Seems he recalled something about a mysterious, little-visited section of Federation-bordered space where starships vanished without a trace, not even leaving behind their log-torpedoes. These unexplained disappearances were infrequent.

All of a sudden, escort duty was beginning to look downright attractive.

"Cicada, that's it, Captain. I'm sure your science officer can supply you with additional information and fill in any details you might require. But briefly, the situation in the so-called Cicada Sector is this: The sector was first reached—but never more than partially explored—over a hundred and fifty terran years ago. Claims to the territory have been in dispute for at least that long, but there appears to be little of value in the sector—certainly nothing worth fighting over has been discovered yet.

"Recent joint discussions with representatives of the Romulan and Klingon Empires reveal that a starship of theirs or of the Federation has disappeared in that sector precisely every twenty-seven point three-four star-years since its initial mapping." She stared into the screen.

"Does that suggest anything interesting to you, Captain?"

Kirk was taken aback. The question was rhetorical. Losing a starship from the fleets of three principalities in a single spatial sector to a sum total of six in a hundred fifty years was unusual, but not startling.

But some eager beaver in Science Center had researched the disappearances and found an uncanny regularity to them. At the very least the inferences one could draw were ominous. Natural disasters rarely operated on so strict a timetable.

"You see what I'm driving at, Captain," the vice admiral continued. "It would be only a slight shift from your current course and you would be able to check out the affected area. Nothing elaborate. Make a casual sweep of a couple of days through the sector, with your sensors wide open.

"Record anything out of the stellar ordinary. You can be in the sector in twenty hours."

Not much use in hesitating. "We'll be happy to do so, Admiral." He paused to scratch a persistent itch behind one ear. All of a sudden, something didn't smell right—something that bothered him and he couldn't pin—ohhhh, yeahhhh!!!!

He stared into the screen. "Uh, Admiral, how long ago was the last disappearance of a ship in the sector in question?"

"Very perspicacious of you, James," she replied easily. She made motions of consulting an off-screen chart. "Ummm, yes . . . it was, I believe, exactly 27.344 star-years ago." Kirk nodded.

"I guessed, Admiral. Your reputation doesn't include deep-space calls to order casual sweeps for anything."

"I had intended to tell you eventually anyway, Captain," she replied—a mite huffily, Kirk thought. "In any case, to observe the formalities, you may regard this as an official order from Starfleet Central. More than those of us at Science Center are interested in these disappearances."

"I have priority override so far as the Carson's World-Bethulia III expedition is concerned. If the ore carrier captains try to make things difficult for you, refer them to me." She smiled wolfishly. "I'll see to it that they get satisfaction. They won't miss you for a few days."

Kirk didn't add that if the schedule of unexplained disappearances in the Cicada Sector held true, they might be missed for more than a few days. But he didn't say that. It could be interpreted in some quarters as insubordination.

Besides, he was getting interested.

"Very well, Admiral. We'll do our best to find your interstellar boojum." Van Leeuwenhook relaxed.

"I know you will, James. Discovery to you!"

The picture of the vice admiral began to fade, dissolve in a shower of confused electrical particles. Uhura's voice sounded over the grid.

"Transmission ended, sir. And just in time, we're nearly out of range."

"Thank you, Lieutenant." He snapped off the viewer and sat thinking. Not that he was superstitious or anything. These disappearances could be due to natural coincidence.

Sure they could, Kirk old chap. Once every twenty or thirty years. But every 27.344 star-years *exactly*?

He was tempted to beam directly to Starfleet Science Headquarters on Vulcan and talk to Admiral Weems himself, but he dismissed the idea as soon as it occurred. Even a Starfleet captain had better be very sure of himself and his reasons before trying to go around a vice admiral—even if only for clarification of detail.

Besides, if something was in the unknown sector that could take Romulan and Klingon ships as well as those belonging to the Federation, there might be valuable military information to gain. The fewer interceptable deep-space calls made on the matter, the better. He worked the communicator again.

"Mr. Spock . . . Mr. Sulu . . . ?"

Both responded. "Spock, I'll be needing a lot of digging from you in a little while. Mr. Sulu, we have a new mission and a new course. Take us to the spatial border of the port sector known as the Cicada region.

"What do you mean you never heard of it? *Tch-tch*, I'm disappointed in you, Mr. Sulu. I thought everyone had heard of the Cicada Sector. Better stay up on your manuals. Mr. Spock will supply you with navigational supplements for cruising within the area. The only charts will be about a hundred-fifty years old, Spock. Kirk out."

Now all he had to do was think out a way to tell the skippers of the ore carriers that their escort was going to take a hike.

VI

Actually it took nearly twenty-five hours for them to penetrate the edge of the mystery sector. No giant galactic monster waited there to devour the ship whole. There were no signs of incomprehensible interstellar weapons manned by unknown races, no all-destroying automatic fortresses ready to blast them from known space.

There were stars in the sector, of course. According to the old schematics some of them had planets. But they were few and far between. They'd been cruising inside the sector for half a day now, and nothing vaguely like a threat had materialized.

"It certainly seems peaceful enough, Captain."

Kirk nodded, tried to relax in the command chair. He couldn't, of course. It hadn't been designed to put its occupant to sleep, but rather to keep him alert.

"How soon will we enter the so-called disappearance zone, Mr. Spock?"

"According to calculations, Captain, we have some thirty seconds to go."

Kirk steepled his fingers on his lap and stared at the main viewscreen. Only interstellar space, spotted with the pinpoints of stars near and distant, stared back. A black ocean, concealing its threats with a sheen of dark beauty.

"All we know," he muttered to himself, "is that ships have vanished in this sector every twenty-seven star-years. A long time for a pattern to hold." He glanced at the helm chronometer. The twenty remaining seconds were up.

"Lieutenant Uhura, place the ship on yellow alert."

"Something happening, sir?"

"No, purely precautionary, Lieutenant."

Uhura felt relieved. Not that she *expected* any trouble, but the regularity of ship disappearances in this area made her more than a little nervous. It didn't seem to bother the captain, though.

Kirk observed the cool demeanor of his communications officer and reflected how fortunate it was that his crew, at least, was not at all worried about this assignment.

"Aye, sir, yellow alert." Uhura swiveled lightly in her chair, manipulated controls. Throughout the bulk of the starship, proper lights changed color, necessary noises yowled warnings.

If there was a lurking, malevolent entity out there somewhere capable of reacting to this gently defiant gesture, it did not do so. Spock checked out the gratifyingly fast compliance of all decks with the order.

"All stations now operating in yellow alert status, Captain." Minutes passed. Still nothing. Kirk began to relax a little. He'd tightened up in spite of himself, but now that they were several minutes into the interference zone and nothing had appeared to volatize the deck beneath him, he felt assured in easing his vigilance.

Nervousness never failed to surprise him. Hadn't he been through all this before? He sighed—tenseness was an occupational disease.

No one noticed Uhura look up sharply from her console. There was a faint, distant sound in her earphones and, no doubt about it, the strange sound had begun the instant they'd crossed into the sensitive sector. But it had been so faint at first that she hadn't been sure.

It was growing rapidly louder, however. And there was no mistaking it for a natural output of any kind.

"Captain, I'm now picking up some kind of subspace radio signal."

Kirk accepted this news calmly, almost expectantly. So there was something here. But a radio signal was hardly cause for alarm.

"Put it on the ship's speakers, Lieutenant. Mr. Sulu, any chance this wavelength might interfere with navigation?"

"It doesn't seem so, sir. It's not anywhere near helm-length waves."

Uhura adjusted her controls. For a moment there was nothing. Then a familiar, wavering tone swelled from the wall speakers and filled the bridge.

It was sensuous, haunting and unmistakably melodic. A deep pulsing beat underlay the melody, a beat that might have been drawn straight from ancient terran drums. The wordless song itself sounded vaguely like guitars and flutes.

It was lovely.

It was rhapsodic.

It was thoroughly captivating.

At least one member of the bridge complement, however, wore an expression of something other than rapture. It was only a source of puzzlement to Uhura.

"It's much more like pure music than an intelligible message, Captain." It grew louder, and she dropped the volume to compensate for the increased power of the signal.

"Beautiful," Kirk murmured. "Might as well let everyone enjoy it, Uhura. Pipe it through the ship."

"Yes, sir." She didn't notice that the men on the bridge

had entered into a state of musical appreciation bordering on Nirvana. They stopped just short of actually swaying in time to the alien rhythm. Even Spock had to force himself to concentrate on his computer readouts instead of on the music.

Helmsman Arex stared at distant stars, his three feet tapping a gentle rhythm in counterpoint to the music pouring over the speakers.

For long moments after the first faint pipings sounded over the speakers there was nothing, nothing but the steady sylphlike strains from the instruments of unknown players. Then Spock looked up from his viewer, surprised.

"Captain, we're being probed."

Kirk spoke slowly, with seeming difficulty. "From where . . . can you trace it?"

"A moment, Captain." Requests were put to the computer. "The signal is apparently originating in a star system some fifteen—no, twenty—light-years distant."

"Any info on it?" Again the library went to work.

A holographed star-chart replaced the speckled blackness of `interstellar space on the viewscreen. Only two planetary systems were shown on the old chart. One glowed with a faint red aura of its own.

"The Taurean system," Spock informed him. "A small G-type star at the extreme edge of this sector. It is the only star for many parsecs thought to possibly hold inhabitable planets. No surface survey was ever performed." The information succeeded in drawing Kirk's attention from the music.

"That's a mighty powerful signal to reach here from that distance," opined Scott. He looked over from the bridge engineering station as the music's tempo seemed to increase slightly . . . abruptly . . . insistently.

"Strange, Captain, I'm sure I'm ascribin' to it something that isn't really there—but it seems to be callin' us."

"It is odd," Kirk murmured. "Yes, I get the same feeling myself, Scotty."

Final confirmation of the signal's attractive power came from the least likely source.

"It does seem to have attributes not unlike a

summons," Spock concluded. Only Uhura was unaffected. She studied the men on the bridge, thoroughly puzzled.

"I don't see any semblance to a summons, Captain." Kirk looked back and replied, rather curtly, she thought.

"Noted, Lieutenant. Lieutenant Arex, set our course for the Taurean system. Warp-factor seven."

Uhura tried to persuade herself that nothing was wrong with any of this. Certainly the alien music was interesting, distinctive—an appealing little tune. But a summons? A distant call to some as yet undefined action? Uh-uh.

She continued to monitor her communications console, but most of her attention was diverted to monitoring the actions of her fellow officers. All of them—Kirk, Scott, Sulu, even Arex, even Spock—wore dreamy, faraway looks. She'd seen similar expressions on the faces of music lovers before. But other forces were at work here, demanding more than mere appreciation from their listeners.

Or was something the matter with her?

It was as if she were the only one who was tone-deaf at a Mozart concert.

No, surely, there was nothing wrong with either her hearing or her sense of musical propriety. But she had to have a second opinion. Pressing a call switch she addressed the broadcast mike softly, whispering.

Not long after her call, the elevator doors divided and head nurse Christine Chapel entered the bridge. She took a fast survey of the room before moving quickly to stand next to Uhura.

"You wanted me, Lieutenant?" she asked quietly, putting a hand on Uhura's shoulder. The communications officer had admonished her to speak softly when she arrived on the bridge—not that anyone else seemed to have noticed her arrival. "Are you feeling all right?"

"*I* am," Uhura replied quietly. She nodded toward the center of the bridge. "But I want you to observe the men here."

"I do that anyway." Uhura didn't smile back. "What am I supposed to be looking for?"

"Just look, see if you draw any conclusions."

Puzzled, Chapel shrugged slightly and turned to comply with the request. She studied her superior officers.

Funny, no one was talking to anyone else. The usual idle chatter that filled the bridge was absent. There was only the strange music that had begun humming from the intraship communicators a little while ago. In fact, everyone present except Uhura seemed transfixed by an unseen hand.

Kirk and Sulu had risen from their seats. They were staring dreamily, distantly, into empty air. Yet their eyes were open and they smiled raptly. Chapel concluded that the music supplied more than aural stimulation.

"Beautiful images," murmured Sulu, confirming her guess.

What images?

Uhura and Chapel saw nothing. The communications officer looked up at her.

"It started the moment we picked up that signal. And it's gotten progressively worse. Look." She pointed towards the library computer station. "It's even affected Spock."

Unlike Sulu and Kirk, Spock remained seated at his station. But he, too, was staring trancelike into nothingness.

Nothingness only to Uhura and Chapel.

"Fascinating," Spock whispered. "Like a Vulcan marriage drum." The shimmering phantom dancing before his eyes began to take on stronger outlines, to solidify in space as his imagination lent it form and reality.

She had shining black hair which fell in silken cascades to her feet, pointed ears, and upswept eyebrows. Jeweled leotards clung to her body like a sparkling second skin. Strands of gems were entwined in that ebony mane, spitting out tiny fragments of rainbow as the light changed.

Now she languorously slid behind a small triangular drum. Her hands, delicate and pale, opened like white flowers. She started to play an unheard rhythm on its taut surface. No, not unheard! There it was now, he could hear it—clear and vibrant as she.

She started to sway alluringly, moving lazily from side to side as she played. Yes, he could hear it, jungle drums accented by picked guitars and delicate Vulcan tassans. But the sound was coming from the intercom, not from the drum, wasn't it? He blinked and spoke thickly. Words came slow and hard, as if he were trying to speak through buttermilk.

"I am experiencing audio-visual suggestion, Captain."

"So am I, Spock." Kirk's tone and attitude had become something less than authoritative.

She was beautiful. Her golden hair was piled high in metallic ramparts, shading a perfect forehead. A gentle breeze nudged the flowing peignoir close to her body, where it clung with maddening intent to high curves and angles.

She leaned toward him, eyes of deep blue staring, warm, inviting. The petals of the crimson flower that lay cupped in her hands opened to him. They were shaped to form a stylized heart.

Kirk shook himself.

"Dimensional visions, too." He frowned. "Any idea what's causing them, Spock?"

The science officer's eventual reply seemed to come from parsecs away. He was still staring, still absorbed in the tugging alien marriage music.

"Logically, we must assume they are a by-product of the scanning probe." All this would have seemed totally crazy to Uhura—if it weren't that everyone was treating it so seriously. But she couldn't keep silent any longer.

"Sir, what visions? We don't see anything." She indicated Nurse Chapel, who nodded agreement.

Somehow Kirk found the reserves to turn from his dancing mirage and look back at them. "Nurse Chapel, you're sure you don't see anything, either?"

"No, sir. Not a thing. What is it you all see?" Kirk ignored her question, turned his gaze to touch in turn on Sulu, Scott, Arex, and Mister Spock. All continued to stare into space, eyes blank and expressions slightly foolish. The image of his voluptuous blonde persisted, and Kirk had difficulty focusing on Uhura.

"Tell me, Lieutenant," he murmured curiously, "have I been looking as silly as that?"

Uhura hesitated, then spoke firmly. This was no time for diplomacy. "Every bit as vacuous, sir."

"Ummm." Kirk considered. It was growing hard to

concentrate. No matter how he seemed to shift and turn, the blonde stayed in his vision.

"Nurse, take a medical reading. Lieutenant Uhura, call Dr. McCoy to the bridge."

Chapel moved away from the communications area and swung her medical tricorder off her shoulder. Since it was precalibrated for humans, she passed over Lt. Arex for the moment and began with a smirking Sulu. No telling what he saw, and she wasn't sure she cared to know.

Meanwhile, Uhura was busy at her console.

"Sick bay . . . Dr. McCoy, please report to the bridge . . . Dr. McCoy, please report to the bridge." She paused while Kirk waited unconcernedly, watching her. Giving him a puzzled look, she tried again.

"Dr. McCoy, report to the bridge—Sick Bay, acknowledge!" Nothing. She looked first at Kirk, then at Chapel, and shook her head. "No response."

"Keep trying, Lieutenant," Kirk ordered dreamily. At the moment he didn't seem to care whether McCoy answered or not.

"Yes, sir."

In the reception office of the *Enterprise*'s central Sick Bay, the communicator call light winked on and off with mechanical patience, while Uhura's voice continued to sound from the attendant speaker. "Dr. McCoy . . . report to the bridge . . . Dr. McCoy . . ."

Dr. McCoy was sitting at his desk. Leaning back in his chair, he had his feet comfortably propped up on same and his arms folded behind his head. At the moment he was staring upwards, but his eyes paid no more attention to the ceiling than they did to the communicator call light. A beatific grin dominated his expression.

Dimly, a part of him was aware of the blinking green light and Uhura's distant, urgent voice. He ignored both with perfect equanimity. His mind was busy with more important things.

"Magnolias in blossom," he sighed. "Magnificent . . . such symmetry of form . . . beautiful . . ."

Uhura gave up trying to contact McCoy. She had a suspicion why he wasn't answering. If she was right, nothing short of general alarm would provoke the slightest response from the good doctor.

For a moment she considered giving the alarm on her own, but she wasn't quite ready to assume the authority. While unmistakably affected by the strange music, Kirk, Spock, and the other officers still seemed in control of their actions. She checked her exterior monitors. The readings they provided were not the ones she hoped to see.

"The probe is getting stronger, Captain." Hands adjusted amplifiers. Also, the rhythmic pulsing had grown more insistent, the melodic convolutions more involved and complex.

"Mr. Spock," Kirk ordered, "reevaluate your scanner readings," Spock's reply was sleepy, but quick.

"I have been doing just that, Captain, though this signal makes normal work difficult. Readings are still inconclusive. That it appeals directly to the subconscious desire is self-evident. But how it relates to the music is as yet undetermined.

"It is odd that only the men appear to be affected by the probe's hallucinatory capabilities. May I suggest that perhaps . . ." His voice trailed off as he stared at the main viewscreen. Kirk was already looking that way.

The faint outline of a world began to grow visible. It increased rapidly in size on the screen. Because of some peculiarity in the ionosphere, the atmosphere had a faint golden hue. As it expanded further, the musical probe grew correspondingly louder—and louder—until it seemed to wash the entire bridge in waves of pure emotion.

The constant driving rhythm defied all Uhura's efforts to keep it at a manageable level. It seemed to emanate now, not from her speakers, but from the walls themselves.

There was a blinding flash of light and the bridge was suddenly bathed in a deep pink glow. At the same time the music rose to a deafening crescendo which momentarily paralyzed everyone. The startling fusion of brilliant color and sound vanished simultaneously.

As the last tints of pink faded from outraged retinas, the probe officially stopped. After the long bolero, the resultant silence was shocking. Kirk, Spock, and the other men continued to stare hypnotically at the screen and the small, brass-hued planet floating there.

"Cut speed, Mr. Sulu, and set us an orbit."

Sulu's reply was casual. "Aye, sir." Kirk rose from his chair and yawned.

"Mr. Spock, we will take a party and beam down to explore the surface. Inform Transporter Chief Kyle of the approximate nexus of the probe-signal generator. We'll try and set down there. Life-support belts, Mr. Spock?"

"It doesn't seem necessary, Captain," Spock replied after checking his scanners. "Everything appears conducive to humanoid life. It doesn't really matter."

Uhura nearly fell out of her seat at that. She could see that Spock's highly uncharacteristic casualness over such a vital question had shocked Nurse Chapel, too. No one else seemed to think it worthy of comment.

"Scotty, you're in charge till we return."

"Hmmm? Oh, okey-doke, Captain." Scott was staring cheerfully at the viewscreen, but Uhura had a hunch the fatuous grin on his face was directed at another sight.

Kirk and Spock left via the elevator. Moments later, they ambled casually into the transporter room. McCoy was already there, and the single security man Kirk had requested, Ensign Carver, arrived shortly after.

"Engineer Kyle . . . Engineer Kyle!" Kirk said, more insistently when the transporter chief failed to respond.

"What?" Kyle raised his head from cupped hands and smiled over at them. "Oh, it's you, Captain. How's things?"

"Pretty good, Chief, pretty good." He moved up into the transporter alcove. "Spock call you before we left the bridge? You can handle those coordinates?" Kyle nodded, grinned at Spock as though the science officer was a long-lost brother.

The other officers joined Kirk in the transporter. Everyone was smiling happily at one another, or at nothing in particular, or at some private thought. After several minutes of this, a touch of reality intruded on Kirk's dreaming.

"I don't want to put you out, Engineer," Kirk murmured easily, "but if you've got a spare moment, could you beam us down?"

"Sure, Cap'. Anything for you."

Fortunately, Kyle had performed this operation several thousand times before. He could have done it in his sleep—and that's just about what he was doing. His mind was not on his job, but he manipulated the transporter controls solely on instinct.

Hopefully, he wouldn't rematerialize Kirk, Spock, and the others a hundred meters above their touchdown point.

On the bridge, Scott moved slowly to the command chair and flopped into it with little grace. His brows drew together. For the briefest of moments he frowned, as if something, something, wasn't quite what it ought to be. Then his previous contentment returned, and a satisfied smile spread across his face. Almost indifferently, he thumbed the log activator.

"Ship's log . . . stardate 5483.8. Chief Engineer Scott in command." For some reason that struck him as particularly humorous. He giggled. Uhura's jaw dropped in disbelief.

"We are continuing to hold standard orbit around a planet in the Taurean system." The world in question drifted on the screen in front of him, holding his gaze. This sight was continually interrupted by other phantoms which flashed across his field of vision somewhere between his nose and the viewer. They tickled his consciousness like bubbles before vanishing, leaving only a thin pleasant memory behind.

Once it was an astonishing orchidlike flower, whose center was a face of delicate elfin beauty. Another time, he saw thousands of gold coins, clinking, tinkling, and bouncing metallically off one another, blowing along a sandy beach like leaves in a high wind. A third time a carved crystal goblet spewed out an endless waterfall of brilliantly faceted gemstones. Now and then, the facets revealed faces that had nothing to do with internal mineral structure.

He continued the entry happily, almost singing the words.

"Probes and sensors utilized subsequent to the departure of the landing party indicate there was once a vast civilization here." The back of his mind wondered if it mightn't be a good idea to report this to Kirk and Spock, down on the surface. Oh well, they should find evidence of same soon enough. Besides, what difference did it make? What difference did *anything* make?

A lithe female form seemed to rise from the contours of a mountain range now visible on the surface below. Ah, lovely, lovely!

"However, life readings of any kind were sparse and concentrated. Captain Kirk has beamed down with others to investigate. Oh, fantastic!" His voice dropped to a whisper even the sensitive log mike couldn't pick up.

There were two poeple on the bridge who saw no orchid faces, heard no wind-scattered lucre, no cascade of jewels. And it worried them.

They were busy at the library computer, intent and agitated. Uhura had been feeding the *Enterprise*'s brain a steady stream of questions. Now she studied the flow of words and figures that formed the reply. Each new answer deepened her frown, increased her apprehension.

"These readings just don't match up with Spock's official report," she snapped. "So far I count three sensor readings that are off—two of them dealing with wavelengths of that probe. That's not like Spock."

She was damning herself now for not sounding the general alarm when she'd had the chance. It wouldn't do much good now. She glanced around at the rest of the bridge.

Sulu was sleeping, head down, on the navigation console. Lt. Arex occasionally patted all three hands together in the manner of a little boy, and Scott—Chief Engineer Scott—was ignoring the still-recording log and conducting a silent orchestra of his own. If she'd seen the instruments involved, even Uhura might have blushed. She used a remote to switch off the log.

No, their reaction to a general alarm would be somewhat less than devastating.

She turned back to the computer. There had to be an explanation buried somewhere in the sensor readings.

There had to be.

The temple reminded Kirk of a well-insulated Parthenon as viewed through a fun-house mirror. Basic architectural lines were there, but they conformed to no known earthly pattern. He couldn't even tell whether the marblelike facing, brilliant white with pink veins and black striations for contrast, was stone or metal. The top of the structure seemed to melt into a pink fog that swirled gently in the light air.

A moment before, several small mist-shrouded forms had coalesced in front of the structure to leave Kirk, Spock, McCoy, and Carver standing just at its base.

It seemed they'd forgotten their life-support belts. Tch! It could have been fatal, but Spock's easygoing assumption as to the planet's congeniality turned out to be correct. By now any outsider would be justified in questioning their sanity, but none of the men affected seemed to find the oversight worth mentioning.

Spock had remembered to bring his tricorder, however. The security guard had one, too, and McCoy had a medical 'corder in addition to his standard emergency kit.

Their gaze never strayed from the temple. They stared in admiration at the arching columns of polished stone/metal, at the delicate, gravity-defying arches.

"Fantastic architecture," Kirk murmured. "Only an incredibly advanced race could have built this place." He didn't seem to find it particularly significant that the temple might be made of stone instead of duralloy or some equally technologically advanced structural material.

His opinion of the astonishingly advanced civilization of this world was echoed by the other members of the landing party. Carver turned to Kirk and gestured at his own tricorder. He appeared to be having some trouble speaking. What was wrong with the enlisted ranks these days?

"You want the routine post-landing checks made, sir?"

"Oh, I don't think that's necessary, Carver," Kirk replied easily. "Why go to all that trouble? There aren't any threats here." His assurance bothered no one. "Spock can handle any required scans."

Fortunately, the science officer's judgment was less affected than the captain's. He was already taking readings.

That didn't keep him from staring at the temple, nor did it make his voice less distant and dreamy.

"There's something compelling about it, Captain."

"Yes." There was no music now, no all-absorbing rhythm pounding in their ears, but Spock was right. Something *was* pulling at them!

Kirk took a half-step backwards and frowned. Spock continued to work with his tricorder and abruptly he also seemed to realize something had taken an unpleasant grip on them.

"Captain, the urgency of the attraction suggests that more than mere visual compulsion is at work here. I advise remaining at a distance until I can determine the depth and significance of this influence. Life forms are indicated—concentrated at some point within this structure."

Kirk's trancelike expression intensified, and the momentary feeling of unease vanished. He seemed to hesitate, looking around for—something. But when his gaze finally returned to the temple, it stayed there—fixed.

"There's no apparent danger, Spock. A belligerent life form would already have sallied out to attack us. Let's go." He moved quickly now, even eagerly, towards the temple steps.

McCoy and Carver needed no urging and followed close on his heels. Spock followed more warily.

It was all very logical, of course. That wasn't the trouble. The trouble was that his logic was leading him down possible lines he didn't care for. But something at work here had a way of muffling the normal lines of reason. Spock almost seemed to have cause and effect tied together, and then everything would sort of blur in his mind.

Huge, intricately carved doors were recessed into the front of the temple. As soon as the men from the *Enterprise* had approached to within a few steps, the doors began to swing silently inward. That in itself should have been cause for greater caution. But Kirk led them inside as though they'd been expected for a long, long time.

They walked down a high, narrow hall which gradually opened into a huge audience chamber. Huge, hammock-like settees filled with silken cushions and high, cube-shaped tables of red-gold were set on both sides of the chamber. Various ornaments and utensils carved from single gems studded the tables and walls.

Always they moved toward a high, cushioned dais at the far end of the chamber. The aliens were there, waiting for them.

Resting on the dais itself or standing in a semicircle around it were a cluster of the most breathtakingly beautiful women any of them had ever seen or imagined. They wore long, togalike costumes which tantilized more than concealed. A few lounged on thick cushions covered with fur.

Like everything else on this world, their skins seemed tinged with a combination of gold and pink. All the colors of the rainbow gleamed in their flowing waist-length hair. Their eyes were a deep, drowning violet.

All stood about two and a half meters tall.

When they eventually moved it was slowly, and with great care and with deliberate patience. The reactions of the landing party were similar.

"Radiant . . . like goddesses . . . such eyes!" came the varied whispered comments. Even Spock was overwhelmed. He did, however, retain enough presence of mind to borrow McCoy's medical tricorder. The good doctor didn't seem to need it.

A quick scan brought some interesting information.

"The form—as is obvious—is humanoid," he murmured. "But there are a number of internal differences of indeterminate significance. Endocrinology especially appears to operate at variance with the humanoid norm. Also, their bodies appear to function at a surprisingly high electrical level.

"According to the tricorder the range of psychokinestatics—outside influences having an actual effect on bodily function—is abnormally high."

"Prettiest body functions I ever saw," McCoy mumbled, utterly enthralled.

For their part, the reactions of the women as they rose and slowly surrounded the men were equally ecstatic.

"They are here . . . such wondrous ones . . . they honor

us with their presence . . ." and similar phrases not calculated to lower the ego of any masculine listener.

It all puzzled Spock, briefly, only because their reactions were exactly what one might dream for. It was
ideal—too ideal. Too perfect. That didn't keep him from
abandoning himself to it completely.

The crewmen had to lean backward to maintain eye
contact as the tallest of the women stepped forward and
extended her hand to each of them in turn. Her voice rang
like prayer bells sounding through Lhasa.

"I am Theela," and the very name seemed to hint of
warmth and love, "the head female. Welcome, James
Kirk, Dr. McCoy, Mr. Spock, Ensign Carver. Welcome,
honored ones."

"Welcome, honored ones!" came the heavenly chorus
from the assembled women.

Kirk mumbled some suitably mushy reply, the sentiment, if not the actual words, echoed by his companions—including Spock. It was fortunate no recorder was
on to set down their words for posterity. Their infantile
responses would never come back to haunt them.

They didn't sound infantile at the time, however. They
sounded delightfully appropriate.

"How do you know our names?"

"The *Oyya* revealed you to us," Theela explained. She
turned to face a shockingly blue curtain shot through with
silver wire. Instead of touching a switch or giving a signal,
she hummed a single soft, distinctive note. The curtain responded by sliding silently aside.

Jutting out from the wall behind the curtain was a large
transparent cube. In its center floated a perfect three-dimensional model—no, not model, a picture, image, whatever label one could think of—of the *Enterprise*. More
perfect than any hologram, it was so real it seemed the
ship itself had been reduced in size and set into the cube.

The landing party moved closer, eyeing the device with
real interest. As an example of alien engineering it was intriguing, but not quite spectacular. Although there were
aspects of it which were unfamiliar—no Federation instrument could produce quite so realistic a depiction, for ex-

ample—the technology required to produce it was not beyond comprehension.

But those few aspects bothered Spock. That, and the sophistication of such a machine in comparison with its basically barbaric surroundings. They did not add up.

"Tonal control," he murmured sleepily. "Quite impressive." Theela moved close and put a hand on his shoulder, looking down at him.

"The *Oyya* will reveal the answer to whatever is asked of it, Mr. Spock."

Spock was skeptical, but before he could ask questions Theela moved away from him to stand next to Kirk.

"We are grateful you heard the signal, Captain, and responded."

Signal . . . there was something about a signal. Something was hammering insistently at the back of his skull, screaming for attention. He shunted it angrily aside.

Signal . . . they were here in the first place because of . . . why were they here?

"That signal—it was a distress call?" Kirk asked.

Theela's smile faded. For a second a terrible sadness seemed to come over her. Then she quickly forced cheerfullness back into her voice.

"I will explain its meaning later, Captain. For now, we have prepared a feast to celebrate your coming—and your safe arrival."

Kirk would have pursued the matter further. He wanted to—it seemed he ought to—but somehow, in the face of Theela's radiant smile and the proximity of her body, the questions lost their initial urgency.

Several women guided each man to one of the swaying, overstuffed hammocks, helped him gently into it. Others brought elaborate golden trays piled high with exotically colored fruits, and white-gold chalices filled with cool bubbling drink.

Two or three women clustered around each man. They began to eat and drink. Especially choice tidbits were chosen for the visitors from the mountain of food.

One swarthy giantess rose and took several round gold fruits from a crystal bowl. "My name is Darah, honored ones," she whispered sensuously. She moved to the center of the chamber.

There she began juggling the fruits while simultaneously starting a wild, barely controlled dance. Performed by anyone else the combination would have seemed ludicrous. But Darah's movements turned it into an incredibly alluring ballet.

Kirk and his companions watched. Theela had knelt at his feet and was stroking his bare legs above the boottops. From unseen instruments, heady music throbbed. If possible, the women now seemed more beautiful, more exotic, more alive than ever. Very much more alive.

"Captain's log," Kirk sighed heavily, not caring whether or not a tricorder was running to pick it up, "stardate 5483.9. The beauty of this place is unequalled. It's the answer to all a man's secret desires, private fantasies, dreams. Exquisite in every way." He paused drowsily and managed to get the chalice to his lips for another sip of the champagnelike liquid.

"We're here to investigate . . . here to investigate." He almost frowned. A last warning tried to sound, faded quietly behind a wall of suffocating pink flesh. "To investiga . . ." Theela made a deft move with her hips, and he smiled.

"The women themselves radiate delight." He watched as Darah continued her juggling dance, moving quickly, easily, back and forth across the chamber floor. McCoy fervently seconded Kirk's unrecorded sentiments.

"Truly, Theela, you are the most beautiful women in the galaxy. But where are your men?"

"They have their own temple, their own compound," the giantess informed him. "We find it better this way. We are thus free to pursue our own pleasures and fulfill our own needs without harrassment from the other."

"I'll drink to that," McCoy bubbled.

Darah, her filmy toga flying in loose folds from her magnificent form, spun across the floor toward them. Suddenly, she called out laughingly.

"Mr. Spock!" She tossed one of the golden fruits toward him.

"I'll drink to that," echoed McCoy.

Spock rose automatically to catch, reeled dizzily and nearly fell over. Theela and several of the other women caught him before he struck the floor.

Kirk was halfway out of his hammock and starting toward Spock, his increasing lethargy finally interrupted by his friend's plight. He got only a few steps before he found himself swaying unsteadily. It finally penetrated the rose-colored haze that had enshrouded him that something was wrong here.

McCoy and Carver were also on their feet, but barely. Neither was in any condition to help anyone but himself. Other women rushed to their assistance.

"Take them to the slumber chambers," Theela directed. "They are tired and heavy with food and drink. They must rest."

There was no malice in her voice, nothing threatening, only honest concern for their well-being. It didn't make sense that they'd been drugged, tricked. And the giantess's reaction was hardly one of triumph.

With a pair of women supporting each of them, the men of the *Enterprise* were led, staggering, toward a side corridor. McCoy managed to gasp something intelligible, but his words were badly slurred.

"Prob . . . probably that nectar, or whatever it was they gave us to drink. It's as potent as Saurian brandy."

"I'll drink to that," mimicked Carver sarcastically. Of the four, he was the last one who should have succumbed to the lure of alien liquor. Some security man! He was blaming himself needlessly. They'd all been fooled.

McCoy looked as if he wanted to say more, but couldn't. Now he was almost wholly under the effects of the powerful drink.

None of them could see very well either. None of them looked back. And so none of them saw Theela staring after them, sadly. Tears were beginning to trail from the corners of her wide violet eyes.

VII

They slept for a long time in the slumber chamber. It was dimly lit, but filled with luxurious furnishings and ornamentation. Kirk lay asleep on an enormous cushioned couch veiled with iridescent black curtains that shut him off from the rest of the room.

A gold headband with a large blue gem set in its center encircled his head. The gem did not sparkle in the dim light. His sleep had been deep, dreamless—but now he found himself stirring and trying to sit up.

The result of these efforts was a wave of dizziness that sent him falling back onto the cushions. A hand moved shakily to his head, touched, examined. He felt the headband. Experimentally he grabbed it as best he could and tugged. The pull failed to dislodge it. It was tight—too tight.

Both hands now. There didn't seem to be any kind of clasp or latch. Maybe he could force it apart along some hidden seam. Useless, it was locked firmly in place.

This time when he tried to sit up he managed it, though it cost him another attack of dizziness. He felt vaguely nauseated. Once more he worked feebly at the headband.

That's when he heard the voice. It was urgent and anxious.

"Jim . . . Jim . . . !"

Funny, that sounded like McCoy. But there was a subtle difference. Even when drunk the doctor's voice had never been that—well, that shaky.

A hand divided the smooth spun curtains. McCoy stood framed in the opening, swaying unsteadily. A headband identical to Kirk's own was wrapped tightly around his forehead. Kirk's eyes widened. His jaw dropped.

McCoy's hair was much thinner—and graying! He

stood now with a noticeable stoop and his face, his face was lined like that of a man of sixty. But an even greater shock was in store.

Spock joined them a moment later. He still stood upright, but there was a definite flutter in his hands. His hair was also tinged with gray. While he definitely looked older, he wasn't in the state of advanced desiccation that had afflicted McCoy. Vulcans generally had a longer lifespan than humans. Therefore the peculiar aging disease had affected Spock less than McCoy.

In the background, Kirk could see a greatly matured Carver. For the first time, he wished he'd brought a younger security guard with them. Even so, Carver was younger than any of them, so it appeared the aging effect wasn't proportional. Carver had aged faster than any of them.

It was almost as if he'd had more to give.

Kirk rose and eyed them in turn, still stunned.

"Bones . . . Spock . . . what's happened to you?"

"Not just to us, Jim," said McCoy quietly in that old man's voice. "You too."

Kirk swayed. McCoy's statement penetrated—not without resistance. His hand came up to touch his own face. His hand—dry, wrinkled. Drier, less supple skin on his cheeks, loose folds of flesh around his neck, under his eyes—lines that didn't belong there. That hadn't been there, hours ago.

He couldn't see the streak of white that ran through his hair, but McCoy told him about it.

"You look about fifty, Jim. I'd guess Spock's artificially advanced age at about the same, though he's got more years to play with than us."

"We've got to get out of here," Kirk stuttered desperately. He'd once seen a man who'd lost his suit on Dryad, the hothouse world in the Demeter system. The man had made it to a survival base. When the rescue team finally reached him, they found only a very large man-shaped fungus spotted with short, sprouting, brown tendrils.

McCoy's seamed face was every bit as shocking.

He started to run for the remembered exit and pulled up, grabbing at his left leg. It seemed that in the past few hours he'd not only acquired wrinkled hands and face and a streak of white in his hair, but also a mild case of bursitis.

He felt unbelievably helpless.

Uhura and Chapel stared down at the readout screen of the main medical computer in Sick Bay. They mentally tried to urge the machine to greater speed. As if in response to their unvoiced pleas, a microtape cassette promptly popped out of the response slot.

Chapel picked it up and both women moved to the desk playback table. She inserted the small plastic rectangle, hit the necessary switch. She spoke to Uhura as the machine automatically rewound the unplayed tape.

"The results of every scan, every probe made by the female science teams. If there's an answer it'll be on this." The accompanying screen winked on and there was a tiny hum as the computer voice activated.

"Computer evaluating." The two officers took a deep breath. "Summation of recent medical and astrophysical scans, with analysis, as per request Head Nurse C. Chapel."

Faint sounds of mechanical life followed. Each second took an hour. Then the voice finally came again, indifferent as it was authoritative.

"Probe is directed at ship from indicated planet, as initially surmised. Probe wavelengths are severely enervating to humanoid males. Prolonged exposure to probe's effects over a long period of time, or if signal is intensified according to figures shown on chart, can cause increasing weakness and accelerated aging to the point of death."

Chapel made a slight strangled noise and Uhura looked stunned.

"At least we've some idea now what we're dealing with," the communications officer said grimly. She directed her next words to the computer pickup. "How do we counter this effect?"

"Countering methodology not available. No projected medical antidote to hypothesized effects. Initiate search?"

"Initiate—and keep advised," ordered Uhura sharply. She moved to the wall communicator as Chapel ran through the figures once again.

"Lieutenant Uhura to Security Officer Davidson." A middle-aged, efficient-looking woman appeared on the tiny intraship screen.

"Davidson here. What's going on Lieutenant? The men in my section have been . . ."

". . . acting like lotus-eaters ever since we entered orbit, I know. I'll explain later, Davidson. Right now I want an all-female security team in the main transporter room as of five minutes ago. All-female security teams are to be mobilized at every entrance to the transporter deck and in the shuttle bay. Anyone—particularly any *male*—who attempts to transport down to the surface is to be placed in protective custody. I don't think any of them will become violent—we've no indications of that so far. But instruct your personnel to be prepared."

"Yes, Lieutenant, but—"

"You and Lieutenant M'ress will be in command of the ship until I return. I'm taking down a security detail myself."

"As you say, Lieutenant." Davidson looked doubtful, but saluted briskly. Uhura cut the transmission and turned to Chaptel; she found the head nurse staring at her with wide eyes.

"What are you planning, Uhura?" The latter was already heading for the elevator.

"I'm taking command of this ship!"

Kirk, Spock, McCoy, and Carver stood in the audience chamber facing the imposing dais. Theela sat there, watching them. Darah and the other women relaxed nearby, also watching. The men swayed weakly, the blue gems set in their headbands now glowing brightly.

Only Spock and Carver were a step above total collapse. Kirk and McCoy were in bad shape.

"We must return," the *Enterprise*'s first officer murmured tiredly, "to our duties on board our ship." Next to him, Kirk frowned uncertainly. He was clearly straining to remember . . . to remember . . . what?

Duties—that was it, duties. He looked up at the staring women. "Duties . . . I have . . ." He stumbled again as the jewel pulsed brightly and had to grab at Spock's arm for support. That arm was not what it should have been and as a result, both men nearly fell.

Theela spoke. She seemed genuinely sorry, no longer adequate consolation to Kirk and his men. "You cannot leave, Mr. Spock," she said slowly, "for you are needed here. As the low waves of the Lura-mag work on your crew, they will come to feel as you do. They are also needed, and they too will join us here."

Kirk drew himself up, finding a last reserve of strength somewhere. "We must go." Turning toward the door he staggered off. McCoy tried to follow and nearly collapsed. Again, it was Spock who steadied him.

"Obstruct them!" Theela shouted.

The other women moved rapidly to form a barrier between Kirk and the other officers, blocking their path to the main exit. Shaking with stabbing, suddenly increased weakness the men hesitated. They had nothing to fight with, their weapons having been taken from them while they slept.

"Together!" Kirk gasped. Somehow they managed to rush the women. But the giantesses grabbed their arms and pushed and dragged them back easily. Their weakness seemed to increase sharply at the physical contact, and they grabbed at their headbands. One by one they slumped helplessly to the floor. On each man's forehead the blue gem shone with appalling intensity.

On the bridge of the *Enterprise*, Engineer Scott lounged dreamily in the command chair. His eyes were focused on the viewing screen and the dreamworld that seemed to be depicted therein. A constant flow of sensuous, beckoning images drifted back and forth in front of him.

The Scottish beret he now wore was tilted at a rakish angle. He was singing an old Gaelic love ballad. Normally, Sulu would have found the rendition distasteful and Arex would have been indifferent. But both seemed to find Scott's performance the greatest musical experience since Gabriel.

Uhrua and Chapel entered from the elevator. The lieutenant's gaze was drawn immediately to Scott. The ballad approached its end as the two officers approached.

She'd been dreading this moment. How would Scott

react? Regardless of any objections, he had to be removed from command—by force, if necessary. In his present condition there was no telling what he might order. She hoped Chapel wouldn't be forced to use the hypo secreted in her belt. There was no hesitation in her voice, however.

"Mr. Scott, as senior lieutenant I'm taking responsibility for the safety of this ship."

Scott turned at these astonishing words and stared up at her. There was an awkward silence. Uhura fidgeted inwardly. Was the strange probe capable of inducing emotions other than pleasure?

Apparently not. Scott merely smiled absently up at her.

"That's very thoughtful of you, luv." He swiveled in his chair and returned his gaze to the viewscreen. Uhura should have been relieved. Instead, she felt only disgust.

"Not as hard as I expected it might be. Damn. Whatever it is, it's really got its hooks into them." She reached around the humming engineer and switched on the log 'corder. Scott made no move to interfere—not that he was in any shape to offer resistance.

"Ship's log, supplemental. Lieutenant Uhura recording.

"Due to Chief Engineer Scott's euphoric state of mind, which precludes effective direction, I am assuming command of the *Enterprise* in the absence of senior officers Kirk, Spock, and McCoy. I accept full responsibility for my actions.

"A detailed account of the events leading up to and dictating this action will be entered later." Off went the recorder and she added to Chapel, "I hope. Christine, until further notice you will serve as chief medical officer."

"Yes, Lieutenant."

In a small chamber somewhere within the main temple, Kirk, Spock, McCoy, and Carver lay stretched out on a huge slumber platform. It was neither as spacious nor as lavishly furnished as their former "slumber chamber." All four were groggy from sleep.

They were apparently alone in the tiny, dark room. There was little light, but it wasn't dark enough to prevent each man from seeing that his companions had aged even further in the last hour.

McCoy's hair was now almost pure white, while

Spock's eyebrows were salted with gray. There were deeper lines in Kirk's face, heavy pouches under his eyes. He rolled over on his side and studied the room.

"They've gone."

"Yes," agreed Spock. Experimentally, he stood, testing his aged muscles. Kirk and Carver imitated him. Spock walked over and gestured at McCoy's waist.

"Your medikit, Doctor. Does it contain anything that might help us?"

McCoy glanced down at the belt in surprise. Sure enough, his compact medikit was still strapped in place and seemed to be intact.

"I wonder why they took everything else and let me keep this?"

"Perhaps because it cannot be used either as a weapon or for communication, Doctor."

"How would they know that?"

"If their question to the device they call the *Oyya* was phrased so as to only indicate those instruments, then the machine would, as is the nature of machines, not volunteer aditional information. We are lucky."

"I have seen no evidence of practical medicine here," the science officer continued. "This entire community of women is a most peculiar mixture of the ancient and ultramodern. No doubt they assume your kit contains only food supplements or hygienic materials."

"They'll be hygienic, all right!" McCoy fumbled at his waist and pulled out a short, thick cylinder with tiny studded dials running down one side. "Cortropine. It ought to help. It's a powerful stimulant—but it'll make its demands later. Not the safest stuff in the world to use."

"There may not be a later if we don't use it, Bones." Kirk slid off the platform. "I'll take the first shot."

McCoy administered a dose to the captain's upper arm. Kirk rubbed at his tingling bicep and began to examine their prison in detail. McCoy continued handing out doses of the fast-working drug to Spock and then Carver.

Kirk found the door, tried it. Not surprisingly, it didn't budge. A close examination of its edges revealed that it was designed to open outward.

"Locked," he offered unnecessarily. McCoy placed the

cylinder against his left arm and gave himself the final jolt. He started to replace the cylinder in the open medical pouch, but Spock stopped him. The science officer began examining the kit's contents with interest.

"What's this, Doctor?" He lifted a thin piece of hinged metal from a plastic tube.

"Portable surgical probe, Spock. The tip's full of impulsors and fragment manipulators."

"Good enough." Spock opened the instrument to its full length and moved to the door. Kirk stepped aside. In response to the captain's unvoiced question, Spock gestured at the door with the probe. "This appears to be a magnetic seal. If so, the slight output of the doctor's probe may be sufficient to disrupt the locking field."

He selected a narrow tip and inserted its slim prong into the nearly flush join of door and wall. Moving it up from the floor slowly, it rose until clicking against something set at eye level. Spock lifted an eyebrow in satisfaction. He activated the tiny power supply.

Nothing happened.

Manipulating it carefully, occasionally activating another setting, he turned and poked the impulsor prong back and forth against the lock.

There was no snap, no sound at all. The door panel moved away quietly, just far enough to let them squeeze out of the room. Spock gave the probe back to McCoy who carefully refolded it and replaced it in its receptacle in the medikit. They might have occasion to use it again.

Spock led the way with Kirk and the others close behind. A surprisingly short walk down the narrow corridor and they came to a thin curtain backed with brilliant light.

Kirk edged ahead of Spock and glanced carefully around one edge of the thin fabric. They were back at the audience chamber. The enormous room was deserted.

Putting finger to lips he led them forward, heading as quickly as he could for the main entrance. The main entrance? Kirk had a disquieting thought.

The doors had appeared to be automatic when they first entered. If they weren't, the four men would have had a terrible time trying to move them manually, even at full strength. He needn't have worried.

When they were less than two meters from the towering stone/metal, the thick doors began to swing aside. Quietly they moved down the outer steps.

Theela chose that moment to enter the audience chamber from a side corridor. She spotted them just as the doors began to close behind the fugitives.

"Assistance, assistance!"

Already the four old men were in the garden that surrounded the temple. It was delicate, tasteful, maintained like a fine clock. However now the polished trees, the neatly pruned bushes, all looked threatening and alien.

Shortly they found themselves breathing with increasing difficulty. The cortropine was beginning to wear off even sooner than Kirk had hoped.

"It's our aged bodies, Jim," gasped McCoy. "The drug is less effective because it has so much less to work with."

They were losing strength rapidly. Already Spock had to assist McCoy. Kirk found himself searching desperately for a cave, an easily climbable tree, any place that could serve as a temporary refuge. But the only asylum in sight was a huge urn magnificently inlaid with ceramic mosaic.

He gagged, cleared his throat. "The big urn, it's the only place!" Then he turned to McCoy.

"Bones, another dose of the drug." McCoy shook a withered hand.

"Another shot in our present condition would be fatal, Jim. Even if I had it."

They hurried to the base of the urn. The curving upper edge seemed to tower over their heads, the smooth convex sides an insurmountable barrier.

"I think I can make it," was all Spock said. He backed off a few steps, took a short run, leaped, and managed to catch one of the big projecting handles near the top. He struggled and succeeded in pulling himself up to a sitting position on the outthrust handle.

A quick glance showed that the interior of the urn was spacious, relatively clean—and empty. It was covered with a heavy metal grid, but they should be able to move that. He locked his legs tightly around the handle and reached down.

With the others helping from below he was able to get

McCoy alongside. They had to hurry. Already the women were racing into the first trees, splitting up to cover the many paths.

Theela noticed a tiny flash of red that was part of no plant. She moved closer and saw it was a piece of torn fabric. Reaching down, she picked it free. No question, it was from one of the alien male's uniforms.

Turning, she cupped her hands and yelled. "Over here, this way!" Without waiting to see if her comrades had heard, she started up the path that curved 'round the bush. Long strides ate distance quickly—and time.

Once, she glanced at the sky. It was growing dark. A typically sudden Taurean storm was coming. The rain could aid the escape of the men. She would have to hurry.

Carver was lowered carefully into the urn. McCoy was let down next. Quickly Kirk helped lower Spock into the waiting hands of McCoy and the security guard.

Then only Kirk was left on top. He unhitched his legs from around the bracing handle and started forward, grabbing for the lip of the rim—he grabbed and missed. His fingers slipped on the slick surface. For a horrible moment he found himself sliding helplessly down the smooth porcelain.

Only a last, desperate grab enabled him to clutch the projecting handle. A supreme physical effort brought him back onto the top of the urn.

"Captain, are you all right?" came Carver's concerned voice. Kirk couldn't spare the wind for a reply. He felt at least a thousand years old.

He made another, more careful approach to the opening. This time both hands got a firm grip on the rim. Pulling painfully and scrambling with his knees, he tried to pull himself up and over.

A sound came to his ears—the sound of running feet, getting closer. That was sufficient to spark a redoubled effort. A final, agonizing pull which closed the heavy grid over the opening—and he fell headfirst into the urn. Spock and Carver barely retained enough strength to keep him from smashing into the unyielding bottom.

Darah and two other women came into the small glade, searching every direction. There was no sunlight left in the gathering darkness to throw an accusing glare off the polished ceramic. The three separated and moved off in different directions.

Feeling more alone than he'd felt in his life, Kirk stood inside the urn and listened to voices and footsteps moving back and forth outside the urn.

"They're not here, Theela," one voice exclaimed. The leader's reply came quickly.

"Come, they might have tried to return to the spot where they arrived!" Footfalls and voices faded into distance.

Inside the urn the officers exchanged relieved glances. That was when Kirk, the temporary respite restoring a bit of his normal alertness, noticed something:

"Our headbands, look at them!" Sure enough, the once brilliant blue gems set in the hellish headbands were now only dull, faceted rocks. They no longer fluoresced with some alien internal heat. The men inspected one another carefully. Not one of the headbands showed a hint of light.

Spock had puzzled over the phenomenon of the glowing gems since he had first become aware of them. He'd formed a theory, and the present absence of light seemed to confirm it.

"I've noticed that the glow diminishes when the women are not present. I believe," he continued, his voice but not his words emotionless, "that they are polarized conductors of some sort, which transfer our vital energy to their bodies."

"Life-force feeders?" queried a doubtful McCoy. "Among some primitive parasitic species it's been noted, yes, but here . . . ?" He looked faintly sick.

Spock nodded. "That is the explanation I can think of which ties our advanced—no, enforced—aging to these devices." He tapped his own headband.

"You may also recall, Doctor, that when we first encountered them, these women appeared slow-moving and listless. But as our own strength has failed, they have become far more energetic and vital."

"More alive," murmured McCoy. "Yes, I see it now. Stupid of me not to see it before. How stupid!"

"Do not blame yourself, Doctor. You are in a far more weakened condition than I. Your powers of observation have decreased commensurate with your physical decline."

Kirk looked thoughtful. "If they find us, Spock, how much longer would we have?"

"It is impossible to tell for certain without a tricorder or medical computer to confirm, Captain, but we seem to be aging roughly ten years per day. More in the presence of the women. This is, of course, only a guess."

No one said anything. No one needed to. Not after McCoy voiced the feelings of all of them in a single, taut sentence.

"Ten years per—in four days we'll all be dead!"

"Dead," Kirk nodded angrily, "and useless to them. Not that they'll care. Theela said the other men of the *Enterprise* would join us. They'll be lured, drawn down here by the probe and the pull of their own imaginations.

"We've got to contact the ship somehow. We must get to a communicator." Kirk put a hand against the hard concave walls and made a testing leap for the rim. He came close, but the effort exhausted him so much that he nearly collapsed. Obviously no one was going to make it out of their hiding place without the help of the others.

"I've retained more strength than any of you," said Spock, stating the obvious. Carver might have disputed him, but chose not to. "My internal system is different, Captain, my life cycle longer. It would be wiser if I go alone to the temple to try and find the communicators and contact the ship."

Kirk found himself reluctantly agreeing. "One man would stand a better chance of slipping past them than four. Still—"

"It is the only logical thing to do, Captain."

Kirk hesitated, searching for a better way. There was no route around the obvious, however.

It took the combined remaining strength of Carver and Kirk to lift Spock until he could grip the outer rim and push aside the grid. McCoy was too weak to offer other than moral support. Somehow Spock maintained his grasp, pulled himself up (pushing the grid back in place so that the others would escape detection) and over the top.

Panting heavily, Spock rested there and surveyed the glade. No one was in sight, for which he was thankful—though he wouldn't have objected, say, to the sudden appearance of a heavily armed Vulcan peaceforcer car.

It took more of his fading reserves to lower himself safely and carefully to the ground. No logic in escaping their refuge only to break a leg in climbing down.

Moving as rapidly as he dared and trying to keep under cover all the way, he headed for the temple. Once a pair of giantesses crossed close in front of him and he was forced to crouch under a bush whose waxy red blossoms he admired more for their concealing size than for their color.

At least the Taureans didn't appear to have an extraordinary sense of smell.

Once again it occurred to him that they seemed in no way up to creating the incredibly advanced sensory equipment which had been used on the men of the *Enterprise*. There was only one explanation: forgotten knowledge was at work on this world.

Spock made it to the temple without further incident. Fortunately the doors were still open. Obviously this was the last place they expected the refugees to return to. The urge to dash inside was overpowering, but he paused long enough to peer cautiously around one huge marblelike pillar. Nothing moved in the vast audience hall.

The corridors branching off from the main chamber also seemed to be deserted. All the women were outside, hunting them. Hunting *him*.

A search of the first, luxurious slumber chamber produced nothing, not a single piece of their missing equipment. A thorough inspection of the central dais from which Theela had greeted them proved equally fruitless. There were plenty of interesting devices around, but none of starfleet issue.

He was getting desperate when he passed the blue curtain concealing the *Oyya*.

If the machine possessed some kind of internal alarm

system to warn of unauthorized users, he'd give himself away. But they had to have a communicator!

He thought, then hummed what he hoped was the right note. The curtain didn't move. He didn't think it would shift aside manually. It was made of metal, not fabric, and looked heavy. He tried again, still with no effect.

But the third whistle seemed to catch the pitch of Theela's voice precisely. Somewhere an ancient piece of machinery agreed. The azure screen slid aside, revealing a now transparent, empty cube. The *Oyya*.

He hesitated. Would it respond to his voice? But Theela had spoken to it in terranglo and as much as offered them a chance to try it.

Answer any question, would it?

"The equipment belonging to the men of the *Enterprise*," he asked firmly, "where is it?"

There was no blur of shifting mists in the cube, no incomprehensible alien visual static. One moment the cube was as transparent as a block of lucite, the next it showed a three-dimensional miniature of a familiar object—the dais at the far end of the audience chamber.

With one difference. There was a panel set into the left side of the platform's base, and it was open in the miniature. Spock wouldn't have known how to replace the curtain even if he'd wanted to. Anyway, he didn't have time. He rushed to the dais.

A minute of frantic exploration around the paneled area revealed a large button set into the metal. He pressed it and the panel cover slid obediently aside, revealing the priceless treasure within.

Tricorders, phasers, rechargers—all their missing equipment was there. He fumbled first for a communicator, frowning when a first grab missed badly. His vision was becoming weaker.

A second try, and the compact instrument was firmly in hand. He flipped it open.

"Spock to *Enterprise*." At that moment he felt rather than saw the crystal in his headband begin to brighten. There was some residual heat put out by it after all. As the glow intensified he swayed, suddenly dizzy. Was he too weak even to talk anymore? Had he even uttered the call?

Uhura's voice echoed back from the orbiting heaven of the starship.

"*Enterprise* . . . Lieutenant Uhura here! Spock, is that you? Spock!" He glanced toward the front of the chamber. There were footsteps.

Several giantesses were just coming through the doors. Apparently they'd failed to locate Kirk, McCoy, and Carver and were returning to ask aid of the *Oyya*. They saw Spock. One shouted and they began to run forward. He tried to shake himself and spoke rapidly into the communicator.

"Request rescue party—all female, emphasize, all female!" "Repeat," he added desperately, summoning his remaining strength. The room was starting to spin. "All female party . . . all . . ."

His knees buckled like soft cheese and he slumped to the stone floor. The women encircled him.

VIII

Uhura was shouting into the communications grid.

"Spock . . . Spock . . . acknowledge! We read you, Mr. Spock, come in!" Dead sound hummed back through the grid. She stepped back, her mind whirling. "Nothing. No, not quite nothing." She activated another switch and spoke again.

"Security Officer Davidson."

"Davidson speaking," came the prompt reply.

"Uhura here, Davidson. I want four of your best women in the transporter room double-quick. Use the ones already there if you think they can handle it. Fully armed. Laser cannon, if they can manage it."

"Yes m'am!" Davidson responded enthusiastically.

Uhura left a bemused Scott—he was humming and bawling something in Welsh now—and headed for the elevator. Chapel went with her, aiming for a different level.

Moments later she reached the transporter room. Subengineer Lewis—Chief Transporter Engineer Kyle being as incapacitated as any other man on board—was in charge.

Chapel arrived shortly thereafter equipped with full medikit and tricorder. The four security girls were equipped with somewhat less benign instruments. No cannon, but Uhura didn't complain. The four were loaded with enough hardware to make themselves sufficiently impolite.

"Transport stations, people. Let's go." She was the first one into the alcove.

Subengineer Lewis outdid herself. They materialized inside the temple, at the far end of the audience chamber. There was barely time to orient themselves. Theela and the other women were waiting at the other end.

The sumptuous settings of the temple interior and occasional strange alien artifacts didn't bother them. They'd all (especially Uhura) been on far more alien worlds, in far more upsetting surroundings. Starfleet security personnel were trained to fight by battling their way through robotic recreations of their own worst nightmares.

What did surprise them was the size of Theela and the others. Women they'd expected, but not giants. Uhura's right hand strayed toward her hip. One burst from the heavy duty phaser strapped there would cut the biggest of them down to size.

The giantesses were gathered around a large transparent cube set into one wall. Apparently the *Enterprise* security team had arrived just in time to upset some sort of ceremony connected with the cube. Certainly the giant women must have been surprised at the sudden appearance of the landing party, but they covered themselves well.

"Greetings," said the largest of them finally, stepping forward. "I am Theela, head female of this compound."

If this gesture was supposed to be conciliatory, it failed. Nor was it intimidating. Uhura took a step toward the bigger woman.

"Lieutenant Uhura of the starship *Enterprise*, head female of this bunch of party crashers. We're here to locate Captain James Kirk and three other fellow crewmen. I have reason to believe they've been treated with something less than total hospitality by you and your friends."

Theela seemed ready with an answer, but seemed to decide that Uhura wasn't about to be bluffed or stalled. "Return to your ship," she said coldly. "You are not wanted here."

"Not until we find Captain Kirk and our friends." Theela motioned to the other women and they started advancing on the little knot of terran females.

"Phasers on stun!" Uhura shouted. "Fire!"

To their credit, none of the women halted their charge. Their courage didn't do them any good. One by one, the stopped-down phaser beams hit them and they dropped to the floor. One got close enough to grab Chapel in a not-so-delicate hand and lift her off the floor before a guard's phaser brought the huge attacker down. Chapel was more stunned than hurt.

They left the giantesses like that, their nervous systems temporarily short-circuited. Uhura moved toward Theela, prodded her firmly in the side with a foot. She kicked a little harder.

Satisfied that the other wasn't faking, and a little upset at herself for the pleasure she was deriving from booting the unconscious woman, she stepped back. Big they might be, but they possessed no supernormal resistive powers.

She gave orders to the waiting group. "Search this place—parties of two. Christine, you come with me." The security teams immediately split up, taking three corridors at a time.

In a tiny side chamber, Spock lay in darkness on a thin bench of unresilient stone. His hidden face was drawn, the lines in it deeper now. But his eyes were open and his breath was constant, if unsteady.

Voices, were those voices? It took a tremendous effort just to raise his head from the stone. Then . . .

"No sign of them anywhere. Keep looking."

That was definitely Uhura! And Nurse Chapel was there, too.

He tried to yell, failed. His body had grown too weak. That left him with one last possibility. Lifting his head higher, his eyes narrowed with effort as he stared toward the door.

Uhura and Chapel found themselves moving down a high, featureless corridor when Chapel suddenly paused. She looked like someone had just hit her with a sockful of wet sand. There was a voice, Spock's voice! But it was in her mind.

". . . nurse chapel . . . nurse . . . chapel . . . ?"

"What is it, Christine?" asked Uhura. Chapel looked bewildered.

"I thought . . . I heard Spock's voice. But I guess—"

". . . CHRISTINE . . ."

There was no mistaking that mental shout! She found her eyes turning frantically to a seemingly blank section of wall. "It is Spock! But how? Of course, Vulcan mind projection. It has to be!"

She moved to stand close to a section of the wall. A quick inspection revealed no hint of latch, knob, dial, or even a seam. She started running her fingers carefully along the dark metal.

"There must be a hidden catch here, somewhere . . . there must be!" Uhura joined her in the hunt. Rapidly the two women went over the smooth surface. No, not completely smooth . . .

It was Chapel who found the slight depression just above her head and pressed inward with her thumb. There was a slight click and a tall, narrow panel pivoted on its axis. They entered a dark room of indeterminate size. The only light came from the hallway they'd just left.

But there was enough illumination to show them the long table. Spock lifted his head once again and tried to speak. As he did so, the light from the corridor struck his face.

Chapel swayed. "Mr. Spock . . . !" Uhura wanted to scream, but that would have been out of character for an acting commander. Still, the calculated suppositions of the medical computer hadn't prepared her for anything like this.

All she could do was ask inanely, "What happened?"

Spock strained to reply but couldn't. He'd been thoroughly drained. He leaned back and closed his eyes, passing slowly from consciousness. Involuntary Vulcan nerves had had enough. This body needed rest. The effort required to generate the successful mind contact with Chapel had exhausted him.

Uhura and Chapel could only exchange expressions of horror.

The urn stood silent in the darkening garden, unnoticed, uninspected. A strong breeze was now nudging branches and flowers with ungentle force. It seemed to lull for a minute, then return suddenly as real wind, a lashing, tearing gale which bent all but the thickest trees.

Sculptured lightning etched copper trails in the gray sky, while alien thunder rolled and echoed back from distant unseen hills. Rain began to fall, slowly at first, fat drops spotting the ground in hesitant, exploring patterns.

Seconds later the storm turned into a raging downpour that would have shamed any tropical rainforest on Earth. Now the reason for the slight downward slant of the garden and temple grounds became obvious. Streams, rivers of runoff vanished down camouflaged, neatly screened holes and into a complex drainage system.

The wind leveled off and blew steadily from the north, but the rain increased, became a torrent, a cataract, falling in solid waves from the clouds. It was a typical Taurean storm, but it would have appalled any terran weatherman.

Kirk, McCoy, and Carver had been lying weakly in the bottom of the urn. Now they found themselves forced to stand as the downpour drenched them unmercifully. The slick sides of the urn provided capricious support.

Each drop seemed to raise the water level in the urn by millimeters. It rose with shocking, alarming speed. And the storm showed no signs of abating.

"We've got to get out of this," Kirk mumbled. The sound of his aged voice barely rose over the splash of accumulating water. Slowly, painfully, Carver struggled to lift Kirk toward the lid of the urn. But their faded strength proved unequal to the task. And the slippery convex walls were unclimbable. They tried again and again. Again and again Kirk slipped back.

There was nothing but to keep trying, to no avail. Ordinarily, their situation wouldn't have been so desperate. Even if they couldn't reach the top all they had to do was tread water until the rising level carried them up. But in their severely weakened condition, such a constant effort might be beyond them.

Even if they did somehow manage to stay afloat all that time in the cramped quarters, it was doubtful any of them would have the strength to slide aside the heavy metal grid covering the top. They might hold onto the grid, press their faces partway through to keep breathing . . . but eventually their grip would weaken, slip, and one by one they'd sink quietly beneath the surface.

Chapel transported back to the ship with Spock and immediately moved the first officer down to Sick Bay. Chapel hoped that just getting him off the planet might help. Initial sensor readings seemed to confirm her hopes, in part. His strength was coming back, but it was still the strength of an old man. His eyes remained closed.

Chapel had been fooling with the headband encircling the first officer's forehead for what seemed like hours. Eventually she'd given up hope of finding a catch. Praying there was nothing automatic in it that would explode on release, she went to work with a surgical laser.

The carefully controlled light removed it neatly. Setting the metal circlet aside she prepared a premeasured injection. The aged body didn't reject the strong medication. She'd been very careful gauging the amount of stimulant. No one on the ship was used to programming dosages for an old person.

Removing the spray hypo from Spock's arm, she set it aside and sat back to watch him. After a few minutes the eyelids fluttered, opened.

"Mr. Spock . . . ?" His head turned. He'd grown no younger, no more supple, but at least he could talk now.

"Instruct female engineer," he coughed, waited till the fit had passed and began again, more confidently. "Instruct female engineer to divert ship's energy to block probe. Use electromagnetic deflectors. Computer will calibrate probe frequency . . . block . . ."

Chapel shook her head slowly. "We tried that, Mr. Spock. It didn't work."

Spock shook his head violently, found the effort nearly blacked him out.

"Don't use normal deflector energies." His voice was growing stronger as the drug raced through his system. "Divert all ship's power into shield. Everything but minimum life-support." His eyes closed but he forced them back open and extended a shaky, withered hand.

"Hurry, Christine." She nodded obediently and turned toward the intercom.

"Get me engineer Sco—" She stopped in midphrase. Chief Engineer Scott was in no condition to program a coffee pot, much less handle complete realignment of the *Enterprise*'s generators. "Get me Subengineer Hondo McDuff."

She nodded with satisfaction. McDuff would handle the complete readjustment of forces with ease—if in her eagerness to satisfy everyone she didn't blow up the ship first.

The women regained consciousness slowly. There was no moaning, no groans at the tingling aftereffects of the phasers.

Theela, the strongest of the group, was already on her feet. Her initial antagonism had gone. She showed no desire to challenge even a tickling phaser effect again.

Instead, she retreated against the central dais and watched Uhura.

The object of her attention waited until enough of the other giantesses had recovered to make the demonstration worthwhile. She reset her phaser while searching around the room, settled on a good-sized, cube-shaped table, and fired.

The blinding phaser beam struck it with impressive force and the solid construct of stone and metal fused into a tiny lump of glowing slag. There was a concerted gasp of horror from Theela and the other women. Uhura's voice had taken on a new intensity, too.

"Release Captain Kirk, Dr. McCoy, and Ensign Carver immediately, or we'll melt your temple down into a pink puddle!" She raised the phaser slightly. "But first, maybe we'll start on you—piece by piece."

Theela didn't reply ... just stood and looked defiant. Trying to exhibit a casualness she didn't feel, Uhura shrugged and raised her phaser the rest of the way, pointing it at a nearby, beautifully worked stone column. Theela wavered, and a restraining hand gestured hurriedly.

"Wait! No more destruction. I do not know where your people are—" Uhura's finger tightened on the trigger, and Theela's tone grew frantic.

"It's true! They escaped, but wait and I shall find them for you. I was about to do so when you appeared."

She left the dais and once again approached the transparent shape of the *Oyya*. The note was hummed and the machine activated.

"I will find your men for you. But first learn of us and the reasons for our actions."

"I could care le—" Uhura began, but Theela was already speaking to the cube.

"The past—reveal it."

Uhura tried to appear unimpressed as a lifelike miniature of a handsome man appeared in the cube. The detail was unbelievable. The man's hair was short, green, and done up in ringlets. Standing beside him a second later was an equally attractive woman, also with hair of green.

"This is the race from whom we are descended," Theela informed Uhura. "They came to this world which you call Taurus when their home world began to die." She gestured around at the silent hall.

"They built this temple and all surrounding it—the automatic food machinery, the gardens, the underground recycling systems ... everything." The image in the cube blurred, then slowly cleared again to revel the man standing alone.

He was changed, shrunken now, old and white-haired and hunchbacked. Theela's voice was sad. "They did not know that radiations on this world drain the life-energy from a body.

"But the women developed a glandular secretion which

partly enabled them to withstand these debilitating effects. It also gave them the ability to manipulate, through special devices and a certain local mineral, the now weakened males—to draw life-energy from them to replace what the radiations stole.

"So in learning how to resist this planet's life-hunger, they acquired that same need. In drawing on the life-force of the men, they caused them to age and die. We are the daughters of those first women. They built the Lura-mag, which draws new men to us, the *Oyya*, and they designed the focusing headbands."

As Theela continued with her tragic history, rain continued to fall. Most particularly it continued to fall into a certain large lump of pottery, in which Kirk and the others splashed weakly, half floating now, their toes bouncing off the bottom. Uhura, as she listened to Theela, had no way of knowing how close Kirk, McCoy, and Carver were to drowning.

"To maintain our long life," Theela was saying, "we must revive ourselves this way every twenty-seven years of your time."

Darah broke in unhappily, "We are eternal prisoners of this need, which we did not ask for. We age very slowly. Our damning immortality has also cost us the ability to bear children. The necessary organs are still there, but they do not function. A by-product of our increased life."

Uhura didn't have to ask how they knew this.

"Why don't you just live out your normal life spans?" asked one of the security guards.

"We have no weapons here, no way to destroy the Lura-mag. And when the men eventually arrive," she hesitated, "we are afraid. We have no wish to be murdered as monsters. We have always feared this would happen were we to confess what we have done."

"So we follow the plan, and the cycle continues."

Uhura muttered to herself. These poor creatures had never known any civilization but their own pitifully confined fragment of history. They'd never known any other way to react, never thought to take the chance of asking for help.

Sympathy later, she reminded herself. They were wasting time—time which might be precious to an aged Kirk, McCoy, and Carver. How precious, she didn't yet know.

"That's all very interesting," she replied honestly. "Now, what about Captain Kirk and his companions? If your fancy crystal ball can locate them, why haven't you done it already?"

"We were about to," Theela reminded, "but you came." She turned to face the cube.

"The men of the *Enterprise* who remain on our world ... reveal them."

An image began to form, screened by plants and vines.

"The garden outside the temple," Theela informed them. The image blurred again, solidified. Then it was as if they were peering at some impossible kind of moving cutaway drawing.

They were looking inside the urn. Kirk, McCoy, and Carver were bobbing inside, pawing at the water which washed over and around them. Kirk and Carver had unsteady grips on the grid covering the urn. Kirk had a grip on McCoy, and his fingers slipped. McCoy slid below the surface as the captain made frantic flailing motions at the water, struggling to reach him.

"They're drowning!" Uhura exclaimed. She turned to face Theela and her hand tightened on the trigger of the phaser. "Where are they? Take us there now, or—"

"The ceremonial urn in the far glade!" the giantess shouted.

Driving, unrelenting rain soaked everything, obscuring their sight for all but a few meters in any direction. The light was dim, except when an occasional streak of lightning shouldered its way between the clouds and threw trees and thick creepers into sharp relief.

Uhura and the security party followed Theela through the nightmarish storm, phasers drawn. Uhura kept hers focused squarely on the center of the giantess's back and stayed close on the big woman's heels.

Back in the temple she'd seemed docile enough, but Uhura was taking no chances on her disappearing suddenly in the darkness. Let her try something—

Without any warning from Theela they burst into the open glade. The urn looked innocuous enough, standing firmly in the high wind. No sign that there were three men floating inside, their lives ebbing away with each passing minute.

"Phasers on third setting!" Uhura yelled over the drumming rain. "Aim for the base!" She was firing her own weapon as soon as she'd given the order.

The concerted low-powered energy from the five phasers struck the base of the ceramic container. Four broad cracks appeared instantly. Water gushed out of the urn as if from four spigots. The sudden release of internal pressure was too much. Cracks multiplied, and the urn split apart.

Kirk, McCoy, and Carver were washed out like wet logs, tumbling and falling over pieces of broken pottery down the slanted muddy ground. Uhura and the other women from the *Enterprise* had shut off their phasers and were rushing toward them even before the flow of water had subsided.

Uhura's face twisted in pain when she saw Kirk. He'd aged even more than Mr. Spock. And McCoy—

"My God—" she muttered, flipping her communicator open. "Uhura to *Enterprise*. Subengineer Lewis, transporter room." The voice of the technician acting for Chief Kyle shot down through the gray clouds.

"Lewis here, Lieutenant."

"Four to beam up, Lewis—and gently, Lewis, gently. We've got some . . . sick people down here."

"Yes, Lieutenant, I've seen Mr. Spock."

Uhura flipped the communicator closed. "Ensign Tadaki, you're in charge. I'm going up with the captain and Dr. McCoy. Vierne, you'll come with me. I'll send you back down for Carver."

"Excuse me, m'am," interrupted Tadaki, "but what about her—and the others?" She gestured at the silently watching Theela.

"If they don't give you any trouble, leave them alone. But if they go near anything more modern than a spoon, or get belligerent—shoot them."

The medtables were waiting in the transporter room. Nurse Chapel was somewhat prepared for the experience of seeing Kirk and McCoy, but her assistants were not.

Nor was Scott, who was assisting Lewis in the transporting.

"Mr. Spock's screen is working," he said in answer to Uhura's unvoiced question. "The rest of the men are recovered, except for some splittin' headaches. Most of us would rather not discuss the whole matter, Lieutenant Uhura."

"Don't blame yourself, Mr. Scott," she replied. "You were acting under an irresistible outside compulsion."

"I still feel a bit of an idiot," the chief engineer grumbled.

"Far be it for me to deny you the pleasure of feeling like one," Uhura admitted. Scott grinned.

Chapel was admonishing her stunned assistants.

"You've seen old men before," she said with an assurance she didn't feel, "get moving."

Drugs and injections restored some strength to the four aged men, but they remained as old as before. Chapel ran test after test on them, took reading after reading. It was a toss-up as to which result was less depressing than the others.

"No results, Captain," she finally had to admit. "The aging process seems to be the real thing, speeded up. I see no way to reverse it. I've . . . I've tried everything I can think of. Perhaps Dr. McCoy—?" Her tone was hopeful.

McCoy's wasn't. "I can't imagine anything you haven't already tried, Chapel." Dismayed silence filled the examination room.

"I'm not ready for retirement," Kirk mumbled. No one laughed.

Spock, who'd lain deep in thought ever since the first injections had refreshed his mind, broke in.

"Perhaps the transporter is the key."

"Key to what?" snapped McCoy testily.

"Our restoration. The transporter computer automatically records the molecular structure of everyone and everything it handles. Humanoid patterns are permanently recorded and shifted to a special section of the library. It's part of the ship's security systems.

"Think, gentlemen, the records of our original forms

were re-recorded when we beamed down to the planet."
Kirk's face showed hope.

"You think, Spock, that if we are transported back to
the surface and then immediately brought back under the
patterns recorded previously, our former bodies would be
restored?"

"Possibly, Captain. It has never been tried before. The-
oretically, a man could be retransported back into his
child's body, if the pattern were available. The danger—
mental as well as physical—has precluded experimenta-
tion in this area. There would not be a second chance."

"I'm not crazy about our chances right now," Kirk replied. "If you think there's any chance at all, Spock—"

"There is a chance, Captain."

Kirk leaned back on the table and spoke to Uhura. "Inform Engineer Scott of our plans and tell him we'll be
back in transporting as fast as," he grinned, "our wheels
will carry us."

"I don't think much of this idea, sir," Scott said when
the details had been explained to him.

"Look at me, Mr. Scott," Kirk ordered. "Every other
attempt to restore our original bodies has failed. This may
be our only chance. You're absolved of all responsibility
for it. It's my decision—mine and Mr. Spock's and Carver's and Bones's. We've *got* to try it!"

"All right, sir, I'll do my best."

"You'll have to, Scotty."

With the aid of Chapel's assistants the four men were
helped into the transporter alcove. McCoy was unable to
stand and had to sit on the transporter disk.

"Go ahead, Mr. Scott."

Scott resisted the urge to draw a deep breath, drew the
levers down. The man glittered, faded and were gone.

There was a beep from the transporter console less than
a minute later.

"We are on the surface, Mr. Scott," came Spock's voice.
"Reprogram the computer as indicated according to the
previously recorded patterns."

Scott delicately shifted four new settings into the transporter control. The settings were crucial and required
matching the new patterns to the old with no room, abso-

lutely no room, for error. He checked it once, could have checked it a dozen times more without being completely satisfied.

"All right, Mr. Spock. Here goes." He began adjusting the proper dials and switches, his eyes glued to one small unassuming gauge set in the console under his right arm.

"I heard them say this has never been done before, Mr. Scott," Chapel whispered. "What happens if it doesn't work, if things don't match up right?"

"If they're a little bit off, lass, just the tiniest bit—then the atomic structure of Captain Kirk, Mr. Spock, Dr. McCoy, and Carver will break up, disperse—scatter to every corner of the universe. And not all the king's horses nor all the king's men will ever put the captain together again."

There was an end to talking as Scott, using more care than he ever had in a transport operation, slowly brought the necessary levers upward. The familiar hum of pattern integration increased. Transporter Chief Kyle had arrived and now stood to Scott's left, double-checking readouts.

"So far so good, Chief."

Four outlines began to shimmer into view, coalesce.

"Easy, easy . . ." Scott murmured to himself.

The outlines steadied, started to take on color—and suddenly began to oscillate violently.

"Scott, we're losing them!" yelled Uhura helplessly.

Scott didn't reply, his hands working faster on the controls. The four outlines seemed to separate into sixteen tiny sections, flutter still more wildly, and then reform into four shapes again.

The oscillation slowed, stopped. Now the humming steadied, and the four outlines began to fill in once more.

"Coming up on zero mark," noted Kyle, only a slight tremor in his voice hinting at tenseness. "Two . . . one . . . mark!" Scott slammed four levers down so hard it appeared sure he'd shove them right through the console and into the floor.

Kirk blinked and looked around. Uhura smiled in relief.

"You're more handsome than ever, all of you." They were themselves again.

Well, not quite.

"That's very nice of you, Lieutenant," McCoy replied, "but why is everyone staring at us?"

"Yes, Scotty, aren't you going to beam us down? It's time we figured out what that probe—" He looked around and a puzzled expression came over his face. "Say, that's odd, Mr. Spock, have you noticed? The music has stopped."

"Indeed it has, Captain. Most peculiar."

Uhura felt like the girl who'd just stepped through the looking glass. "What's going on here? Aren't you glad to be back in your own bodies again?"

Kirk looked at her strangely. "Back? I don't remember having left mine anyplace, do you, Bones?" McCoy shrugged, looked innocent.

"I think I know what's happened," mused a thoughtful Scott.

"Well, I wish you'd tell me," pleaded a badly confused Uhura.

Scott turned to her. "It's simple, lass. The captain, Mr. Spock, Dr. McCoy, and Mr. Carver are once again as they were before they first beamed down to the planet. That not only includes their youthful looks, it includes their original brain patterns, which include memories. They've lost some time—and experiences."

"What's all this, Mr. Scott?" queried Kirk, stepping off the platform. "Why the delay?"

"It's kind of complicated, Captain," began Scott. "We have some tapes from Spock's tricorder, plus those from Dr. McCoy's and Ensign Tadaki's, which ought to clear things up . . ."

It took only a few hours for the four repatterned officers to relive the experiences of the past day. It was difficult to get used to, but the tapes didn't lie.

McCoy didn't stay for all of them. He had a number of questions of his own to put to the medical computer.

Eventually he handed Kirk the results of his work.

"Aren't you going to handle it, Captain?" asked Uhura.

"No, Lieutenant. Besides, I think it might mean more coming from you. I don't have any particular desire to go back down to this particular world. Not if what happened to me on those tapes really happened. It was like watching yourself acting out a bad dream."

Uhura nodded sympathetically. "I understand, Captain." She turned and headed for the transporter room.

Theela, Darah, and the other giantesses were overjoyed when Uhura announced the results of Dr. McCoy's research. Not that they were in any position to reject the offer, she thought sardonically, but she had to admit that they accepted it with what seemed like honest relief.

Theela led her to a large concealed room behind the temple dais. It was dominated by a seated console and an incredibly complex arrangement of cables, glowing globes, and objects of unknown purpose. The entire apparatus pulsed with internal radiance and hinted of concealed power.

"The Lura-mag," explained Theela solemnly. "Our blessing and our curse." Uhura drew her phaser and set it on high. But before she could begin the work a huge palm came down gently on her forearm. She glanced up at Theela.

"No, let me. It is my place."

Uhura hesitated, but the look in the giantess's eye seemed real, even anxious. She handed over the phaser.

Theela could only fit a fingernail over the trigger, but she managed the tiny weapon well enough. In a few moments the Lura-mag had been reduced to a quietly hissing mound of molten plastic and metal. Theela turned and quietly handed the phaser back to the watching Uhura.

"Tell Captain Kirk we have kept our part of the agreement."

Uhura nodded approvingly. In spite of herself, she was beginning to feel sorry for these poor, bloated creatures.

"There are major medical facilities on Kinshasa. We'll take you there." She noticed that the other women had appeared in the doorway and were watching expectantly.

"How soon will we become as other humanoid women?" asked Theela.

"Dr. McCoy says it should only take a few months. The same modified estrogren that increases your life-spans abnormally is also responsible for your exceptional size, it seems. Certain operations are possible ... bone reduction, for example, to partially correct this. You'll still be unusually tall, but the differences will be more manageable."

A new life—a normal life—perhaps love." She smiled down at Uhura, who didn't know whether to cry or throw up. "There are many different kinds of immortality."

That expression, at least, Uhura could empathize with.

As expected, McCoy's declaration that the Taurean women would be able to lead a normal life was somewhat optimistic. The arrival of the dozen spectacular beauties on Kinshasa created something of a sensation. Their reception at the Federation Fleet Hospital was rather different from that normally reserved for sick aliens.

The doctors professed they were only interested in studying the endocrine irregularity that seemed to prolong life—but Kirk suspected that more than scientific curiosity motivated the male portion of the staff.

In any case, it looked like the Taureans were going to have few troubles gaining acceptance in the Federation. They might be regarded as a challenge, it seemed, but not a threat.

PART III

THE
INFINITE
VULCAN

(Adapted from a script by Walter Koenig)

IX

"Captain's log, stardate 5503.1. Escort of the Carson's World/Bethulia ore shipment having been assigned to other vessels, the *Enterprise* has been ordered to survey a new planet recently discovered at the Federation-Galactic fringe."

Kirk clicked off and stared at the fore viewscreen. The journey out from Kinshasa had been peaceful and uneventful. Now an Earth-type world with a normal scattering of clouds, seas, and brownish land masses filled the screen.

He wasn't surprised Starfleet Command had diverted the *Enterprise* from escort to survey duty. The discovery of a potentially colonizable unclaimed world took precedence over any but the direst emergency. It was interesting, pleasant duty. And if Vice-Admiral van Leeuwenhook had pulled a few strings to get the *Enterprise* the choice assignment, well, it was only a reward for a job well done.

It was imperative to make an official survey and lay claim to the world quickly—before the Klingons, say, or the Romulans discovered it. Inhabitable worlds were not all that common, and competition for expansion was fierce.

Furthermore, this globe seemed to be a real prize to the astronomers using the Moana predictor. Not only did preliminary orbital scans insist it was inhabitable, it checked out as downright lush—a garden world.

Everything seemed to point to a choice discovery, just waiting for her first load of Federation settlers—until Sulu's surface probes located the city.

129

"Inhabitants, Mr. Sulu?" That would be the end of any colonization.

Sulu's expression was uncertain. "No intelligent reading, sir. But it's hard to be sure. There's such an abundance of lower life—plants and small animals—registering that it will take time to sort out any intelligent forms. One thing's certain, if it's a major metropolis, it sure isn't overcrowded."

"I'd rather not wait for secondary analysis, Mr. Sulu." Kirk rose from the command chair. "Mr. Spock, Dr. McCoy. You'll accompany Mr. Sulu and me on the landing party. Mr. Scott, you're in charge."

"Aye, sir."

Kirk headed for the door. "Scotty, buzz down to security and have them send along a couple of people to go down with us. This kind of life-form density implies the presence of predators as well as grazers.

"Yes, sir," Scott acknowledged as he slid into the command chair.

The party of six assembled in the transporter room with admirable speed.

"Put us down near the center of the city, Mr. Kyle," Kirk instructed the transporter chief. "If there are inhabitants I want to meet them right away. It's always best to size up the local populace before the high muckamucks come running with official greetings."

Kyle nodded. His hands moved on the controls.

The city was magnificent.

Wide green spaces alternated with soaring angular structures that looked more like idealized cathedrals than functional buildings. Spires and glasslike towers were laced together with a network of arching bridges and spunsugar roadways, many fading to near invisibility in the bright sunlight.

The metropolis was constructed along gigantic lines, everything built to proportions four times human scale. Yet it was a place of beauty and grace.

It was also dead.

No policeman panicked at their appearance. No busy citizen halted in his daily stroll to gawk at the alien magicians who had materialized beside him. No curious crowds gathered 'round, and no one notified the local president, chief, or leading hooligan.

Dead.

Weeds, vines, and something like a thick terresterial seaweed had made the city their own now. Even the shiniest, newest-looking structure was clothed in a blanket of climbing greenery. Greenery, and less wholesome looking plant life.

They began walking toward what they estimated to be the center of the city. Sulu and Spock were busy making continual tricorder readings.

"Life readings are still confused, sir. I can't sort them out, yet."

"There is something else, Captain," added Spock. "I am getting a sensor reading on some form of generated power—" He looked around and after a moment's search, pointed ahead. "From that building."

"Let's check it out," said Kirk. He was at once pleased and disappointed. Pleased that there seemed to be no barriers to development of this world, and disappointed at the thought that the architects of this dream city no longer existed. They walked toward the structure in question.

Sulu paused a moment, trying to recalibrate his tricorder to screen out another identified low-life form. Then he frowned and glanced skyward.

The sun glare blocked out his view of . . . what? He thought he'd heard a flapping sound, but they'd seen no animals on this world yet. When the dots cleared from his eyes he looked again. The only sky riders were clouds.

Hmph. He took a step after the others, glanced downward as he set his foot—and stopped. The tiny plant looked like a sporing dandelion. Moving his tricorder close he took a standard reading. Results were anything but. Unaware of the fuss it was causing, the fuzzy, delicate top of the plant quivered slightly in a gentle breeze.

"Well, now, what's this?"

The building the others were approaching appeared to be well maintained. Surprisingly well, Kirk thought. Perhaps the city wasn't as dead as it looked. Here was one structure that the mosslike growth and other climbing vegetation hadn't encroached. Its front walkway was clean, the window ports all intact and throwing back the morning sunlight.

"Captain, Captain!"

Kirk and the others whirled. Ush and Digard, the two security men, moved their hands toward their weapons.

"What is it, Mr. Sulu?"

"You're going to have to decide for yourself, sir." He had come up to them. Now he stopped and pointed to the ground near his feet. Everyone looked down.

There was nothing there except some smooth gravel set in a layer of earth—and a single fluffy, fuzzy little growth. Looked like a dandelion, Kirk mused.

"How long," he asked gently, "has it been since you've had a long leave of duty, Lieutenant? I thought Valeria was enough for anyone, but—"

"No, sir, really, look!"

The helmsman took a couple of steps to one side. There was a tiny popping sound like a foot pulling out of mud as the fuzzy raised itself off the ground. It scurried on miniature roots after Sulu. As soon as it reached his side—how it could tell where it was was another mystery—the root endings promptly made like a corkscrew and burrowed contentedly into the earth.

Kirk's stare was incredulous. If it wasn't so undeniably alien, the fuzzy would be downright funny.

"What is that thing?"

"It's an ambulatory plant. When it stops, it takes up new residence. The little fellers are all over the place." He moved back to his first position. The fuzzy popped, skittered after him, and repeated the rooting operation.

"I think it likes me."

Kirk shook his head. "We always encourage our officers to make friends with the natives."

"I always did think your personality was kind of wooden, Sulu," said McCoy idly.

"That's fighting dirty, old bean," the helmsman countered.

"It's a good thing they're *not* intelligent," Kirk observed.

"Captain," Spock broke in, looking up from his tricorder, "I dislike interrupting your amusing byplay, but that power reading now gives evidence of being an electronic probe of some sophistication. I believe we are being scanned."

Kirk's phaser came out, and the others reacted seconds later.

"Phasers on stun—stay alert. Mr. Sulu, Mr. Digard, stay here. Mr. Ush, come with me, please."

Kirk, McCoy, Spock, and the second security man moved toward the building. Sulu watched them go anxiously. But when time passed and nothing leaped out to blast the earth from under them, he quickly lost interest. He found his gaze dropping down to the friendly fuzzy.

Obeying an impulse, he knelt and picked it up.

"Ow!"

Well, what—Friendly, indeed! He dropped the plant quickly, shaking his finger to try and relieve the pain. He examined the injured digit with concern. The fuzzy, as if unaware that anything unusual had taken place, burrowed back into the soil.

Sulu mumbled to himself. "Must have been a thorn. Oh, well."

The entrance had no solid door. Instead, the opening doglegged to the left and out of sight. Moving cautiously, they edged around the U-shaped portal. It opened without warning into a gigantic room.

No, the room wasn't gigantic in itself. It was just that it was built to the same four-times-human scale as the city. Like the building's exterior, the room was clean and orderly. Lights on panels and consoles flashed on and off. There was a constant hum from powerful, hidden machinery. It looked very much like a laboratory.

There was no longer a question about the city being dead. Everything about the room suggested constant, everyday use. Spock gestured toward a towering wall panel flecked with odd-shaped switches and knobs.

"The probe originates in this instrument wall," he informed them, checking his tricorder. "As does an incredibly powerful force-field shield. I cannot imagine the purpose of the wall instrumentation, but the presence of the force field indicates that someone does not want it tampered with."

There were several high shelves in the wall next to the panel. The lower ones held, among other things, a pile of alien yet still recognizable cassettes filled with scrolls of tape. One scroll cassette sat in a playback slot. Spock pulled it out and began examining it closely. Nothing appeared to object to this sudden manipulation of the cassette.

McCoy was busy with his medical tricorder. Suddenly he looked up in astonishment.

"Jim! I'm picking up a humanoid life-reading of incredible strength. It's as if it—"

"EEEYAAHHHH!"

The agonized scream came from outside the chamber. Readings, tapes, everything were forgotten as they raced for the street. Spock absently slipped the cassette into a pocket.

Sulu was stretched out on the ground. His arms and legs were splayed wide apart and rigid with unnatural stiffness. No one had to ask what was wrong with him. He was almost totally paralyzed. Only his eyes made frantic motions.

Ensign Digard stood alert and gripped his phaser tightly, hunting for some unseen enemy to use it on. McCoy swung his medical tricorder around on his shoulder and knelt beside the motionless helmsman.

"What happened?" he asked Digard.

"I don't know, Doctor!" The guard's voice was wild. "I didn't see a thing. I was standing here, watching the entrance you went into, when Mr. Sulu just—screamed, all of a sudden, and fell over."

McCoy studied the first readings on the tricorder. His words were curt, clipped.

"He's been poisoned. Some kind of nerve toxin. Composition unknown, naturally."

He nudged the tricorder aside and skillful hands worked at the small containers in his belt medikit. A narrow tube was produced. McCoy didn't even bother to roll up the helmsman's shirt sleeve, simply jammed the tube against his upper arm.

Pulling it away, McCoy proceeded to check a tiny gauge set into the side of the metal pencil. His frown deepened and he reset an all but invisible dial below the indicator. Again he pressed it to Sulu's arm, paused, and pulled it away. A second check of the gauge and McCoy seemed to slump slightly, shaking his head in frustration.

"Can you help him?" Kirk had to break the choking silence.

"I don't know, Jim, I don't know. Blast! I can't get a correlation with any known venom." He shrugged sadly. "Either they're too alien to affect your system and they don't bother you at all, or else you run up against something like this." His head jerked towards Sulu.

"Antidotes are always found—after the first few autopsies."

Kirk tried to sound hopeful. "Maybe the ship's medical computer can . . . ?"

"Forget with the medical computer!" McCoy snarled. "He's got two minutes to live, unless I can find an answer." He muttered angrily to himself.

"Anaphase . . . synopmist . . . dylovene . . . maybe dylovene." The ineffectual tube was returned to his belt and a slightly larger instrument substituted. A quick adjustment of the hypo setting and then it was applied to Sulu's other arm.

There was a gentle hissing sound. McCoy pulled the hypo away and waited. After a few seconds he took another reading with the tricorder, concentrating on the newly treated region.

"No good, it's no good," he husked. "Soon the venom will reach his vital organs. Dylovene takes too much time to work . . . assuming it would work—"

"Maybe a stronger dose," Kirk urged.

"That won't be necessary," came a soft, pleasant voice. A new voice was about the only thing that could have turned their attention from Sulu at that moment. They spun to face the direction the voice had come from—the entrance to the laboratorylike building.

Five beings stood there. Their only similarity to man or Vulcan was in the question of size. Beyond that superficiality, they were utterly alien.

Their heads—Kirk presumed those faintly oval shapes topping the rest of their bodies were heads—were partly covered with a fine furry bristle. Two waving eyestalks were the only visible projections. There was no hint of a mouth, ears, nose, or any other recognizable external sense organ.

The bodies themselves were composed of a tight bunching of slender, ropelike extensions, some of which seemed to hang loosely at their sides like a long fringe. Other extensions grouped tightly together near the bottom before spreading out into a haphazard assortment of bulbous protuberances. Kirk guessed that these served as motive limbs for the creatures. This was revealed as so when they started to approach the landing party.

Their color was an ocher-yellow-green—not especially healthy-looking, but for all Kirk knew, the local version of a good tan. Perhaps they regarded Kirk's own fleshy-pink as a sign that he was nearing the last stages of desiccation.

Despite the complete strangeness of their appearance, Kirk felt none of the revulsion toward them that some more humanoid aliens could produce. Maybe it was their apparent passivity. They showed no sign of caution or of the usual wary belligerence.

If anything, they seemed inherently peaceful.

They got another surprise when the leader of the group spoke. Not only were the words intelligible, they were downright smooth. The tone was quiet, reasoned. Resined, Kirk thought idly, wondering at the ability of the human mind to make jokes in the most unfunny situations.

He noticed out of the corner of an eye that Spock was taking a discreet tricorder reading on their visitors. The first officer's diplomacy might be ineffectual. The aliens might be perceptive enough to tell what he was doing. On the other hand, they might ignore Spock if he walked three times 'round their leader, bumping him with the tricorder.

Still, as with any first contact, it didn't hurt to be as tactful as possible. There were other things on Kirk's mind at that moment, however, which made attention to protocol difficult. All he could blurt out was, "Who are you?"

The being leading the group—who was a little taller than his four companions—replied softly.

"I am called Agmar. I believe we can help."

Kirk nodded once and turned away from him—if it was a "him." He kept his voice low as he murmured to Spock.

"What are you getting on them? Who are we dealing with here, Spock?"

"A moment, please, Captain. Give me a little time. The information I have thus far obtained does not permit a reasonable answer yet." He made an adjustment to the tricorder.

Meanwhile the five aliens had moved to surround the unmoving Sulu. The leader, Agmar, bent over the unconscious helmsman—a smooth, supple movement, like a reed bending with the wind.

Jointless, that explained it. Agmar and his companions moved without the stiffness of human joints.

Hovering motionless over Sulu, the eyestalks studied the prone form for several seconds. Then one of the free-hanging limblike extensions moved out from Agmar's side to extend over the body. A drop of some viscous liquid was extruded from the green tip.

McCoy, who'd kept a watchful eye on the whole sequence, now felt obliged to step in.

"Just a minute. I can't let you . . . whatever you are . . . inject him with some—" he hesitated, momentarily flustered, "—alien tree sap!"

Agmar's reply took no notice of the implied insult. "To wait is to assure your friend's death." A single eyestalk swiveled independently, like a chameleon's, to stare at McCoy. "I must proceed."

"Bones—" Kirk put a restraining hand on the doctor's shoulder. "Let them help."

"All right, Jim. But I don't like the whole idea." He turned away and strolled over to where Spock was still working with his tricorder.

"An interesting discovery, Doctor. These beings are of botanical origin."

"Intelligent plants?"

"So it would seem."

The loose tentacle dipped lower. With a gentle touch,

Agmar applied the drop of golden liquid to the side of Sulu's neck. Now both eyestalks turned to observe the watching humans.

"It is a powerful antidote, quickly absorbed. He should begin to respond momentarily."

"Of course," suggested McCoy, still a little miffed, "it's of a completely alien nature and may not have any effect on him at all."

"True, Doctor," Spock agreed, "yet the same could be said of the poison which has so obviously affected him. I see no reason why the antidote should be rejected."

"Thanks," was all Kirk could think of to say to the creature. It rose, repeating the same supple movement.

"Welcome to the planet Phylos."

They certainly seemed friendly enough. A fraternal greeting and a badly needed helping hand, all in the first moments of contact. Still, he wasn't quite ready to fall all over himself in an orgy of backslapping. He'd been on too many worlds where the obviously black had turned out at the last moment to be white, to the detriment of the unfortunate caught in the color change.

But until given a reason why, he would treat the Phylosians as friends.

"I'm Captain James Kirk. This is Mr. Spock, my first officer; Dr. McCoy . . ." He went on to identify the rest of the landing party, including the motionless Sulu.

"You seem to have been expecting us, Agmar."

A tentacle (limb?) fluttered in the direction of the laboratory building.

"Our instruments have scanned and tracked you since your vessel first entered our space, Captain. We had reasons for not revealing ourselves immediately to you. But the injury to your companion compelled us to shed our hiding.

"We are a peaceful people, and we have a fear of aliens." The Phylosian spokesman seemed to hesitate. "We have had unfortunate meetings with such in the past."

Kirk nodded understandingly, glanced over at Spock.

Role reversal was always difficult. *They* were the aliens, not the Phylosians.

There was a movement on the ground, and he found

his attention drawn back to Sulu. The helmsman was still prone, but no longer motionless. He was starting to squirm like a man waking from a long sleep.

"What happened to him, anyway?" His touch of professional jealousy now long forgotten, a curious McCoy spoke while kneeling near Sulu and running his medical tricorder over the helmsman's chest. Scientific interest had taken over.

"He was bitten by the Retlaw plant. It is deadly only if the wound is left unattended."

"Mobile plants seem to be the rule on this world, rather than animals," Kirk observed, hoping he wasn't treading on someone's religion. But Agmar took no offense.

"That is so."

"Your medication worked quickly."

Agmar didn't shrug—he couldn't, having no shoulders—but Kirk felt he could sense the equivalent.

"A minor achievement."

"Minor achievement!" blurted McCoy, looking up in disbelief from his tricorder readings. "I never saw an antitoxin work so fast. I don't know anything about your other sciences, but if this is a 'minor' sample of your medical capabilities, I'd like to chat with some of your doctors."

"Doctors?"

"Physicians—healers."

"Ah," Agmar exclaimed. "Yes, Doctor McCoy. I understand now. But you must realize that healing is not a specialized function among my people."

"Not special—" McCoy looked incredulous. "You mean you're *all* doctors?"

"Not in the way you mean, Doctor McCoy. But each has the ability to ... to repair a number of damaged bodily functions. We will talk of this more, later, if you wish."

"I wish, I wish!" McCoy looked rather like the little boy about to be let loose in the candy store. A low moan from Sulu precluded further conversation.

The helmsman's eyes were open, and he appeared to be making motions of getting up. McCoy made another pass with the tricorder. Then he looked up and nodded. Amazement still tinged his words.

"Something's destroying the poison left in his blood-stream, all right. Body functions are running up to normal. And I mean running." He glanced at the Phylosian leader.

"Look, Agmar. Agreed, if the poison affects humans, a local antidote conceivably might. Clearly does, in fact. But how could you be so sure it would work?"

"We could not be sure," the Phylosian replied softly. "But there have been humanoid aliens on Phylos before. Besides, it was the only chance left for your friend."

"Humanoid aliens who spoke our language?" asked Spock.

"Ah, you are curious as to our method of translation and communication. The voder, a mechanical translator." He reached into the folds of his central body area. For a fleeting moment Kirk expected him to remove a mouth.

Instead, Agmar produced a small, round, flat disk of metal. When he "spoke," his voice came from the center of the disk.

"Our natural organs of verbal communication are quite small. They require a great deal of artificial amplification to be effective any distance. The voder is completely self-contained and most efficient for this purpose."

"Most," agreed Spock, hoping for a chance to take one of the unbelievably compact instruments apart.

Such charming exchanges of mutual admiration were fine, Kirk reflected, but right now other things concerned him more.

"I like puzzles, Agmar, but I also like answers. We were pretty convinced when we first set down in your city that there was no one here. Then we find you—or rather, you find us. Yet I find it hard to believe that the few of you are the sole inhabitants of this metropolis. We're not exactly standing in the middle of a local desert. Where are the rest of your people?"

"Your curiosity does your profession credit, Captain Kirk, and it shall be satisfied. Come with us and we will show you."

Kirk looked down at Sulu. With McCoy's help, he was struggling to his feet.

"How do you feel, Mr. Sulu."

The helmsman blinked. "I'm ... I'm all right now, Captain ... I think. One moment I was sucking my finger and the next—wham!" His voice was that of a man waking from a dream and finding it reality. "I felt like an incendiary grenade had gone off inside me."

"Can you walk?"

"Yes. I'm okay, sir." Sulu straightened himself.

"All right, then." Kirk turned back to Agmar. "Let's go."

The Phylosian turned—perhaps pivoted would be more accurate—and ambled off in the direction of the building next to the laboratory. His companions, none of whom had yet ventured a word, turned with him. Kirk and the other bipeds followed.

"You sure you're all right, Sulu?" pressed McCoy.

"Fine, Doctor." The navigation officer even managed a slight smile. "Hard to believe now that there was ever anything wrong with me."

McCoy shook his head and muttered to himself. "Remarkable ... crazy and remarkable ..."

"Yes," added Spock softly. "How fortunate for us that Agmar and his fellows were so close by."

"You said it!" agreed McCoy fervently. Something scratched at his mind, and he gave Spock an uncertain glance. But the science officer gave no sign that his words meant anything but what they said. He speeded up to come alongside Kirk.

They entered the building, turning first through another of the unbarred but mazelike entrances. Inside they found themselves in a hall of titanic proportions stretching endlessly into the distance. The metal walls rose to form a domed ceiling high overhead. A skylight running the whole length of the enormous corridor was set into the curving roof.

Agmar stopped. Kirk slowly turned a full circle before returning his attention to the alien.

"Well, where are your people, Agmar?"

Instead of answering, Agmar went to a panel set in one

wall and depressed several hidden switches. There was the slightest hissing sound. One security guard reached instinctively for his phaser and looked properly abashed when no threat materialized.

A tall, high door slid aside in the nearest section of wall. Row upon row of glasslike cases, looking like so many rectangular diamonds, filled the revealed section.

No one noticed Sulu put a hand to his head, and he covered the gesture of weakness quickly. McCoy and Spock moved down the ranked glass caskets while Kirk followed curiously. Agmar and his four companions remained in place, watching. Presumably this necrophilic display held no surprises for them.

The leader of the aliens gestured with a limb. There was a hint of sadness in his voice.

"Our people, Captain Kirk."

Each individual sarcophogus was nearly ten meters high. A single gigantic body filled every crystal coffin. And each of the immobile forms was covered from head to root with a covering of thick green bristle.

They had no recognizable heads, not even of the kind Agmar and his friends had. Instead, at the top end of each shape was a mass that looked something like an artichoke. But under the bristle, Kirk and the other crewmen could see that the actual bodies were composed of the same furry ropelike extensions, also bunching up tightly near the base and spreading out into footlike protrusions. In this respect they were identical to Agmar. And there were other resemblances between the living Phylosians and these embalmed giants.

It was an impressive and rather chilling sight.

Eventually Spock looked up from his tricorder. "Nerve tissue mass is exceptionally high. Readings indicate these beings utilized almost seventy percent of their brain capacity—a very high ratio."

Kirk turned and looked back at Agmar. "Your early ancestors."

"No," replied the Phylosian, "only the generation before us." He bowed slightly.

"Then what happened?" Kirk prodded. "I never heard

of such enormous physiological changes taking place in such a short span of time."

Agmar's voice was matter-of-fact.

"A human came to Phylos."

X

Kirk hesitated. It was too late to back out of the question now. "You mean a humanoid?"

The eyestalks were angled directly at him. "No, a human—like you, Captain. You remarked on the reaction of humans to the poisons and antidotes of our world. Such things can operate both ways, Captain James Kirk.

"The human, quite unintentionally, brought sickness and death with him—mostly death. But instead of running away, of taking flight and leaving us, he remained and worked to try and save us from the very disease he had carried."

McCoy gestured with his medical 'corder. "It adds up, Jim." He nodded at the silent sarcophogi. "The bodies all show evidence of gram-positive bacteria. It's carried by humanoids without ill effect, but preliminary readings taken when we first landed indicate that Staphylococcus strains aren't native to this world. It must have been like the worst plague imaginable."

"We had no way of knowing what was destroying us," confirmed Agmar. "That, I think, was the most horrible thing of all to our forebears."

"*Was*," McCoy echoed. "You were alive then?"

"Very young we were and barely formed, but yes, we remember that time."

"Then how? . . ." Kirk paused. There was a new sound in the room. He thought he'd heard it before, somewhere. Something like wings flapping.

There was a louder sound, and he looked upwards. A

rush of air slammed at his face and he ducked instinctively. He got the impression of something streaking past just in front of his nose.

The creature didn't fly away. It remained hovering overhead, circling in the still air of the corridor. The intruder was a good twelve feet long. It's segmented body was hinged in the middle and the upper half would swing awkwardly from side to side.

Despite the flapping sound, the beast had no wings. In place of them, a pair of thick coils protruded from the body. The creature dipped slightly and the coils contracted, kicking the floating monster powerfully upwards once more. It repeated this maneuver regularly.

The constant contractions produced the flapping sounds. Those coils looked taut as steel and reminded Kirk of something much less benign than a bird's wings.

"Plant life, Captain," Spock informed him. "If there are animals here they are surely scarce. These creatures appear both primitive and aggressive."

Abruptly, the whooshing sound was repeated as the thing dove again at Kirk. He took a couple of halting steps to one side and dodged just in time. Out came his phaser, down went the trigger, and . . .

Nothing happened.

He tried again. Nothing. The phaser wasn't putting out enough heat to warm a piece of old toast.

"Your phasers!" Spock, Sulu, McCoy, and the two security men tried their own weapons.

"They won't work on any setting, sir!" said Sulu nervously.

"To insure the preservation of the forebears there is a weapons deactivator in effect here," Agmar told them. "Your destructive devices will not work."

McCoy yelled a warning. "It seems to be after you, Jim!"

"Weapons deactivator," Kirk murmured, keeping a careful eye on the darting movements of the, well, swooper was an apt term. "Then *this* should work." He pulled out his communicator. "Kirk to *Enterprise* . . . Kirk to . . ."

It might as well have been an invitation. Suddenly the

hall was filled with the big creatures. They didn't appear out of the walls, but they seemed to.

Half a dozen of them immediately ensnarled Kirk, before he could complete the call. He struggled, and the communicator bounced to the floor.

"Captain!" Sulu shouted. The others moved toward him and drew their own attackers.

Spock was enveloped quickly. Something fell from his pocket—the tape cassette he'd picked up earlier. No one saw it fall —certainly not Digard and Ush, who were busy with attackers of their own.

Meanwhile Kirk was fighting back with plenty of vim, and absolutely no effect. Something knocked his legs out from under him and he found himself pinned to the floor like a trapped butterfly. He struck out with a hand, contacted nothing. The darn things were quick as well as strong.

It was over as soon as it had begun. Kirk, Sulu, and the others lay motionless on the ground, held tightly in the grasp of dozens of swoopers.

Sulu, who appeared to have recovered from one attack just in time to succumb to another, looked over at Kirk.

"What to you think they have in mind for us, sir?" Kirk didn't answer his helmsman. Instead, his attention was riveted on action overhead.

"Something tells me we've just been the prize suckers for a diversionary assault. Look!" Other eyes went upward, to see Spock, totally enmeshed in swooper coils, being flown 'round the bend near the building's entrance.

Another shape intruded on Kirk's vision and stared down at him quietly. If anything, Agmar's attitude was apologetic.

"I am sorry for this deception, Captain Kirk. But there was no other way."

It was Kirk's task to remain patient and understanding of alien mores. Right now, however, he'd have taken considerable pleasure in soaking Agmar and his fellows in oil and vinegar and tossing them to death.

He wrenched with all his strength at the bar on his right arm, but the swooper coil encircling his upper torso was as unyielding as an anaconda.

"What are you babbling about, Agmar? What are those things going to do with Spock?"

"He has been chosen to serve a great cause," the Phylosian intoned reverently. "The Master has waited many years, searched many visitors, studied many nearby worlds in hopes of finding a specimen like Spock. It is good." Agmar raised a loose fold of himself skyward.

The swoopers immediately released Kirk and his companions—reluctantly, it seemed—and took off at top speed down the big hall, melting away into hidden corridors and side panels like a cloud of bats in a cathedral.

"And now," continued Agmar, "all the worlds of the galaxy will share in total peace and harmony!"

There was, of course, a time and a place for anything . . . including a little educative violence. At the moment Kirk felt like sharing peace and harmony about as much as he did partying with the Phylosians.

He climbed slowly to his feet and approached Agmar with just such unharmonizing thoughts in mind. The eyestalks would be a good place to begin, he decided.

"So help me, Agmar, if you don't tell me where Spock is, I'll . . ."

He broke off as an enormous shadow spread across the room. It wasn't a swooper. Kirk looked up. The sight was at once more familiar and more alien than any they had yet encountered on this greenhouse world.

Standing in the doorway was a human male. He was perfectly normal in every way save one; he stood just under twenty-four feet.

He wasn't smiling.

There was a movement immediately in front of the landing party, and Kirk lowered his gaze. Agmar and his four associates had fallen to their knees—or knee-substitutes—before the giant. It was the most humanlike gesture they'd yet made. The implications of the movement were appalling.

McCoy had the presence of mind to activate the medical tricorder at the giant's entrance.

"Praise to the Master!" the five Phylosians chorused dutifully. "All praise and adoration to the Restorer, the Master, our Saviour!"

"Another plant?" Kirk asked quietly. This one would be hard to swallow.

But McCoy's 'corder insisted that in this case, at least, appearances were not deceiving.

"No, it's definitely human, Jim. That explains that first unusual reading I picked up." Further explanation was soon provided by the giant himself.

"I AM DR. STAVOS KENICLIUS #5," the giant boomed. He wore only a short pair of pants and several instruments. A cane or walking stick the size of a small pine was clasped in his right hand. "WELCOME TO PHYLOS, CAPTAIN KIRK."

"No thanks, Keniclius. Yours is the second welcome we've received here and I'm getting sick of them. I don't want any more of this world's hellos."

"DO YOU KNOW WHAT YOU DO WANT, CAPTAIN KIRK?"

"You bet I do. Where's Mr. Spock?"

"THAT IS NO LONGER ANY CONCERN OF YOURS, CAPTAIN." The giant took two strides toward them. "HE IS MINE, NOW. MORE IMPORTANTLY, THE ESSENCE OF HIM IS MINE. I HAVE WAITED FOR MR. SPOCK A LONG TIME . . . TOO LONG TO CONSIDER GIVING HIM UP."

"RETURN TO YOUR SHIP."

He bent and picked up the communicator. It looked like a toy in his massive palm. He tossed it contemptuously to Kirk, who caught it automatically.

"HERE IS YOUR COMMUNICATIONS DEVICE. GO BACK TO YOUR SHIP."

"Not without my first officer." The two men glared at each other.

If Spock had been present he'd undoubtedly have advised against a confrontation between Kirk and a man four times his size and more so in weight.

Kirk might have thought of it himself, except that he was subject to human traits which did not trouble Mr. Spock. Right now, for example, he was too mad to consider the situation dispassionately.

"I AM SORRY, CAPTAIN. YOU WILL LEAVE NOW OR SUFFER THE CONSEQUENCES." He made a gesture with one hand.

A flock—no, a crop—of swoopers came darting into the chamber again. Pausing overhead like a swarm of organic

helicopters, they circled back and forth over the knot of
watching humans. Their hinged bodies jerked in the middle, twitching nervously from side to side.

Dropping his gaze, McCoy happened to notice the tiny
tape cartridge Spock had dropped earlier. He bent and
picked it up, slipping it without undue motion into a
pocket. His caution was unnecessary. Both Keniclius and
the Phylosians had their attention focused wholly on Kirk.

The object of their study stood fuming silently. He was
frustrated, angry, and almost mad enough to take on the
huge Keniclius despite their difference in size.

But he'd already had one very enlightening experience
with swoopers and their abilities while they were operating
under external restraint. He had no illusions about the
outcome if Keniclius let them run loose.

For now, then, they had only one choice. He flipped
open the communicator and raised it slowly to his lips.
There was always the chance that either Keniclius or the
Phylosians were thought sensitives. No, if that were the
case they should have fallen dead from reading his
thoughts several minutes ago.

"Kirk to *Enterprise*," he repeated. "Chief Kyle? Beam
us up."

Kyle was smiling when they materialized normally in
the transporter room. His smile turned to a worried frown.
It deepened as the little party exited the alcove. He made
a frantic grab for certain controls.

Kirk took a moment to reassure him. "Easy, Chief, you
haven't lost Mr. Spock."

"Well, then," the transporter chief replied, searching the
room, "where is he?"

"Out of reach of your transporter, I'm afraid. For the
moment. But you might keep hunting for him. Try the
transporter on his pattern every now and then in the area
of our touchdown point. There's always the chance something down there will get lazy, or move him, and you'll
suddenly be able to bring him aboard."

"The power drain, sir," began Kyle, but Kirk cut him
off.

"We have plenty of power, Mr. Kyle," he said as he

headed for the elevator, "but a distinct shortage of Mr. Spock. Try at five minute intervals."

"Aye, sir," Kyle agreed uncertainly. His acknowledgment barely beat the closing doors.

Kirk held a small, quick conference to explain the situation to those principal officers who'd remained on board. It was a solemn group of men and women who stared expectantly back at him when he'd concluded.

"Uhura, you'll have to take over the library computer station in Mr. Spock's absence. Lieutenant M'ress will manage communications for you."

"Yes, sir."

"I want you to use the library to dig for two things, Lieutenant." He ticked them off on his fingers. "One, any record extant of a form of plant life of extraordinary intelligence and a technology so advanced they don't bother to boast of it by visiting inhabited worlds."

"And two—I want you to check into the one hope we have in all this."

"Hope, Jim?" McCoy looked puzzled. Kirk only smiled back confidently.

"A giant who is fool enough or megalomaniac enough to tell us who he is." He looked back at Uhura.

"A human named Keniclius—Stavos Keniclius. Said individual may or may not be entitled to the label of doctor." Uhura nodded and moved rapidly to the library station. Seconds later its console was a Christmas tree of blinking lights.

"Sulu, you and Arex get to work with the ship's main sensors. See if you can locate Spock or Keniclius. And Sulu, see if you can program some sensors to differentiate the Phylosians from the lesser plant life. They're probably the only other intelligent life forms on the planet." Both helmsmen moved to their stations and began to work swiftly.

That left only McCoy.

"Sorry I can't help, Jim."

"You can, Bones." Kirk slumped in the command chair. "While Uhura, Sulu, and Arex are running checks, you can get yourself down to Sick Bay and find me a nonnarcotic, nonenervating tranquilizer. If I don't relax soon

I'm going to start breaking things. And I haven't got time for a trip to the therapy chamber." McCoy grinned.

"I'll see what I can find, Jim."

He wasn't gone long. And by the time the mild relaxer had taken effect, Kirk was able to speak with more patience and listen with a little of the same. Inside, though, he was still seething.

"Anything at all, Mr. Sulu?" The helmsman shook his head.

"We haven't been able to pick up anything like a humanoid life-reading, sir. And it's not because they're attempting to decoy or divert our probes—there's no evidence of any surface interference. Spock and Keniclius must be somewhere our sensor scans can't penetrate."

"Outstanding news," Kirk grumbled. "What about the Phylosians?"

"It was hard to calibrate for an intelligent plant form, sir. We're registering thousands of botanical readings in the city, including the swoopers, which have a definite pattern. But no sign of anything higher. Nothing that might be Agmar or his friends." Kirk frowned, thinking. "Agmar said something about a weapons deactivator in operation in at least one of their buildings . . . but nothing about its range or limitations. Let's find out. Mr. Sulu, lock ship's phasers on that laboratory building we first entered. Wide area stun setting."

Sulu manipulated controls. "Ready, sir."

"Just a minute." Kirk turned to face Uhura. "Lieutenant, how are you coming on information about Keniclius?"

"There's nothing current, Captain." She looked disappointed. "I think I may be getting something from the biography section of the recent history bank, but it'll take a moment or two, yet."

"All right, Lieutenant. Keep at it.

"Fire phasers, Mr. Sulu." Sulu hit the proper switch.

"Firing, sir."

A beam of pure energy erupted from the bowfront of the *Enterprise*. Instantly it disrupted orderly molecules, surprised combinations of oxygen, nitrogen, carbon, and a host of others as it speared down through the atmosphere of Phylos.

Nothing could stand before that paralyzing beam, powered by the space-warping engines of the great starship. Nothing solid—

Sulu was staring into a gooseneck viewer. Now he turned to look back at Kirk.

"No effect, Captain. Nothing at all. Phaser stun was neutralized at . . ." He paused and checked another gauge set into the console near the viewer, "A distance of approximately one thousand meters above the target area. Should I try a stronger setting?"

"No." Kirk drummed his fingers on an arm of the command chair, and thought.

"I suspect it either wouldn't have any effect at all, Mr. Sulu, or else it would break through and destroy anything it touched—Mr. Spock, too. That means that either way our weapons are effectively useless. All right. We'll have to go back down there and rescue Mr. Spock without them."

"The old oriental martial arts are kind of a hobby with me, Captain," said Sulu. He smiled faintly. "But I don't think hands and feet will work too well against those swoopers."

What, exactly, is a flash of genius?

Mental stimulation. A concatenation of cerebral crosscurrents. The fusion of one particle of cause with another of effect which—once in a while, just once in a while—produces a molecule of solution.

But all McCoy said was, "I think there might be something we can use that'd be more effective, Sulu." A crooked smile crossed his face. "I'm just not sure which section—"

"If you've got any suggestions at all, Bones—" By way of reply, McCoy leaned close and whispered in Kirk's ear. The Captain's expression grew by turns amused, disbelieving, and finally determined.

"Where'd you get an idea like that, Bones?"

McCoy looked grimly pleased. "From Agmar."

"I don't know—" Kirk mused. "I see what you mean about 'which section.'" Turning suddenly he hit an armrest switch, spoke into the broadcast grid.

"Kirk to engineering. Scotty?" The chief engineer's filtered voice replied from the other end of the starship.

"Here, sir."

"Scotty, I've got a priority project for you. Who's your weapon's specialist?"

"That'd be Lieutenant Chatusram, sir."

"Get him. I've got some special equipment I want you to make up—and I want it yesterday."

The special equipment was basically very simple. McCoy had no trouble conveying what was needed over the intercom. Nor, according to Chatusram, would it be difficult to make.

"I don't think we'll have any problems with the actual construction, Captain," explained the weaponsmith, "though some of the nonsolid components may take some time to compose. The ingredients are simple, but the combination required is not. Still, I'm sure my staff and I can manage it."

"Good for you, 'Ram," said Kirk. "Mr. Scott, see that the lieutenant gets all the help he needs."

"Aye, Captain."

"How soon, Lieutenant?" Chatusram's reply was cautious, but confident.

"I believe if the basic mechanical components are in stock, within the hour, Captain."

"That'll have to do. Hop to it, gentlemen. Kirk out." He ended the discussion.

It was Uhura's turn to speak. She's been waiting impatiently throughout the cross-ship conversation and now she broke in before anyone else could demand Kirk's attention.

"I have the requested information on the man identified as Stavos Keniclius, sir. I'll put the statistics and what visuals there are on the main screen."

"Thank you, Uhura." Kirk turned back to McCoy. "Bones, you really think this gadget of yours will work? It seems almost too simple."

"I can think of several reasons why it should, Jim. That's one of them. Another is what Agmar said that gave me the idea in the first place. The clincher is that, way back when, my great-granddaddy had the finest gar-

den in metropolitan North-South America." Kirk nodded
and looked to the viewscreen.

The screen lit, and the feminine computer voice of the
Enterprise sounded over the speaker.

"Working."

"Here it comes, sir," said Uhura. Almost before she finished, a portrait had appeared on the screen.

There were some slight differences—the figure in the
portrait was slightly older, for example—but Kirk, McCoy,
and Sulu recognized Keniclius's features immediately.

More revealing was the accompanying statistical chart,
especially those figures which declared that the man
shown was a normal human of about the same height and
weight as Kirk.

While they studied the printout, the computer voice
supplied additional information.

"Drawn from recent-near-recent Earth history file, cate-
gory scientists, male, subheading iconoclasts ... Keniclius,
Stavos. Terran physiologist-physicist period Eugenics
Wars. Specialist in eugenics and manipulative endocrinology. Noted for plan to clone perfect humanoid prototype
as founder of idealized 'master race' to act as galactic
peacekeepers. Concept evaluated by ruling government of
time and formally rejected as, quote, 'too antihumanistic.'

"Experiments persisted despite governmental decree.
Upon discovery of continuance of illegal research, Keniclius banned from terran community. Voluntarily accepted total exile and vanished into an uncharted region of
space. Cursory search initiated. No body found, no official
death certificate issued—"

The computer droned on, pouring out additional information. Most of it was trivial, peripheral and, more importantly, downright unhelpful. There was nothing that
might be employed as a psychological weapon against the
giant below.

But they'd pegged Keniclius, all right.

"No further data," the computer concluded. Voice and
visual display disappeared together. Then McCoy spoke.

"Wasn't there an old story about a modern Diogenes
roaming the galaxy in search of someone special?"

"Someone special," Kirk muttered. He looked up. "A

perfect someone. Someone special to begin the ideal race, yes, I've heard that story too, Bones, as a child."

"That's just it, Jim. This can't be *the* Keniclius. He'd have to be over two hundred and fifty years old!"

"The original Keniclius, yes," Kirk noted. "Keep in mind what the library just told us. What was he banned for?"

Understanding lit McCoy's eyes. "I remember now. He said he was Keniclius 5. My God, he's gone and cloned *himself*, to carry on his search! And his clones have re-cloned themselves, right on down the line." He shook his head, an expression of mixed distaste and admiration.

"At least we're not dealing with a complete megalomaniac," Kirk added. "If we were, he'd long ago have decided that *he* was the 'perfect specimen' all along. Then we'd be faced with an army of giants instead of just one."

"I'll grant that in his favor," admitted McCoy reluctantly, "but by the same token, Jim, he's not going to be an easy man to talk out of his dreams. . . ."

XI

Forty-two point one five minutes later (ship-time), Kirk, McCoy, Sulu, and Chief Engineer Scott assembled in the main transporter room. Scott carried three small traveling bags in his arms. He handed them out to his fellow officers while Kirk tried to regard the upcoming attempt with a detached air.

"It's seems incredible that a man could take a few cells from his body and successfully reproduce himself time after time. Yet that seems to be the kind of disturbed genius we're dealing with in Dr. Keniclius and his oversized successors."

At the moment, however, Sulu had other things on his mind than the astonishing feats—biological or other-

wise—of their giant antagonist. Most of his worries concerned the untested quantity resting in the leather carry-
bag. He hefted it and tapped the contents. It responded
with a faint metallic ring.

"I just hope these things work, that's all."

"Oh, they'll work all right, Lieutenant," Scott assured
him. "The equipment's simple enough—foolproof, in fact.
Chatusram and I saw to that. But I admit I've got my own
doubts about the stuff they contain. I've heard of some
mighty strange ways to fight aliens, but—"

"These are mighty strange aliens we're fighting, Scotty."
Kirk moved into the transporter alcove. "As soon as Dr.
McCoy, Mr. Sulu, and I have beamed down," he told the
chief engineer, "I want you to leave orbit and—"

"Leave orbit, sir?"

Kirk nodded. "If they think we've gone, I have a hunch
they'll stop scanning the area around their still-functioning
structures. On any other world in a similar situation it
would be standard precautionary procedure to keep scanners on. But the Phylosians do whatever Keniclius tells
them to do, and this mutant is so confident of his own
power—he's been a virtual god for so long—he won't
think any mere humans like us will dare defy him.

"He's been out of touch with humanity too long to be
anything but contemptuous of it. Not that I can blame
him, considering what some of us were like during the Eugenics Wars. Give us thirty minutes on the surface, Scotty,
and then circle back."

"All right," the chief engineer reluctantly agreed. "But
if I may be permitted an opinion, sir . . . I dinna like it."

"Neither do I." Kirk made sure he was well inside the
perimeter of the transporter disk. "But without phasers or
any other modern weapon, we'll need all the surprise we
can muster. If the ship seems to leave, we might get it."

McCoy and Sulu joined him in the chamber. He turned
to look at the waiting chief Kyle.

"Energize."

The three men became three drifting masses of lambent
color. Then they were gone.

Scott stared into the empty chamber for a moment, became aware that Kyle was watching him.

"Well, what are you starin' at, Kyle?"

"Nothing, Chief. I—"

"See that you don't do it again."

"Yes, sir."

Scott stalked off toward the elevator doors. He'd have to officially assume command now—and it would be he who would have to issue the unpopular retreat order.

Life was dreadfully unfair sometimes!

Three glittering cylinders resumed human shape on a street of the Phylosian metropolis. Sulu was checking his tricorder as soon as they'd fully rematerialized. He kept the mysterious leather bag tucked tightly under one arm.

"No indication of a scan, sir," he said finally. "I don't think they know we're here. Unless—"

"No," Kirk sighed gratefully. "That kind of subtlety is beyond Keniclius. If he knew we were back he'd show up roaring biblical pronouncements, or send a crop of those toothy fliers. Let's get a move on."

Kirk took two steps and started to turn the corner around the thin tower they'd set down next to ... and almost walked straight into a flight of the just-mentioned swoopers.

Flattening themselves against the curving wall in the convenient shadow of the glass edifice, they barely breathed as the swarm of powerful carnivores sailed past.

"I'm not sure I can take too much of this," McCoy finally gasped. "Watch those predictions, Jim. Why'd you take me anyway, instead of Arex or a couple of security personnel?"

"You ought to know better than that, Bones. We don't know what kind of shape we'll find Spock in."

"If we find him," murmured McCoy.

"Let's not even think about that, hmm?"

Sulu looked up from his tricorder and tried to inject a more hopeful note. "I wouldn't worry too much about those swoopers, Doctor. They seem to be almost mindless. They attack primarily as a reflex action."

"Out of sight, out of mind, is that it?" McCoy grunted. The helmsman nodded.

"The way is clear now, Captain."

They turned the corner without being challenged. Moving at a smooth trot, they headed for the laboratory building.

Once, a tiny dandelionlike plant tried to follow Sulu. It took Kirk and McCoy several minutes to catch up with the sprinting lieutenant. Other than the single fuzzy, they encoutered nothing ambulatory.

They'd materialized in a different section of the city than the first time. If only they'd landed here initially, events might have taken a different course. But that was wishful thinking. They turned another corner.

Came up short.

"I don't believe it," Sulu murmured.

"Incredible," was the only word Kirk could think of. McCoy just stared.

They were standing close by the entrance to a colossal, hangarlike building. The structure was easily a couple of kilometers long. Inside, ranged neatly in double rows, were hundreds of translucent, milky, teardrop shapes, each dozens of yards high.

In the immediate foreground were the five Phylosians. Each rose on a small, automatic lifting platform. They were working at the teardrop shapes, cleaning them, scraping and pulling a thick mossy growth from their sides.

"What else could they be but ships, Jim?"

Kirk agreed. "Looks like they're getting ready to go on a trip, too. But where? To what purpose?"

"By the number of ships here I'd say a mass migration is being planned—or invasion."

"Agmar insisted they were a peaceful people," Sulu put in.

"Oh, sure!" spat McCoy sarcastically. "We've had ample evidence of that, haven't we? 'Peaceful' has almost as many definitions as love, Mr. Sulu."

"Is that a clinical opinion, Doctor?"

"Ease off, you two," warned Kirk. "We'll probably have a definition supplied, soon enough." He looked thoughtful. "But you've got a point, Bones. These ships, this city—I'm not saying the motives and abilities of a vegetable civilization would be so different from ours, but let's not jump to any conclusions. This is the first one we've encountered."

"And the last, I hope," the doctor muttered. He added, half to himself, "I always did hate vegetables as a kid. Now I know I had a good reason."

"And that's about enough hilarity, Bones. If Spock were here he wouldn't be laughing."

"Sorry, Jim." McCoy turned serious once again. "I'd almost forgotten why we're here." He nodded in the direction of the gigantic hangar. "Those ships look like they've never left the ground. Probably they were all set to leave, when Keniclius the first arrived and his new diseases swept the planet."

Kirk nodded, glanced at Sulu. "Any indication of Keniclius's or Mr. Spock's whereabouts?"

Sulu checked the tricorder, looked disappointed. "They're not around here, sir. Certainly not in the hangar. I read only the Phylosians."

"Umm. Well, followers can be led. Maybe we can be as persuasive as Keniclius."

Moving from wall to wall and taking care to conceal themselves well, they gradually made their way to the entrance of the enormous structure.

It appeared that each Phylosian was taking care of one ship by himself. That was fine with Kirk. It would make the momentary disappearance of one of their number less obvious to the others.

Agmar was working close by. At the moment he was filling the tank of his lifter with some sort of cleaning fluid from huge canisters stacked neatly against the near wall. Taking up positions behind these, the three men waited for the leader of the Phylosians to return.

Two others came and filled their tanks before McCoy whispered tensely, "Here he comes!"

"Do we want the flitter he's riding?" asked Sulu hurriedly. Kirk shook his head.

"Might take too long to figure the controls. I'd rather stay on the ground anyway. It might be subject to outside orders. I don't want someone yanking my feet out from under me a couple of hundred meters up in the air."

Agmar brought the little vehicle down smoothly to the

canisters. His back was to them. They tackled him without any trouble.

Sulu and Kirk were momentarily repulsed at handling a creature who felt like a clump of sticky straw. They almost lost control of the struggling alien.

Fortunately, McCoy was used to handling things that would turn many men squeamish. He wasn't at all bothered by the unconventional feel of the Phylosian. He hung on tightly until Kirk and Sulu had recovered from the initial shock of contact.

They had no difficulty dragging him back behind the high containers. Kirk's only worry had been the chance that the repair flitter might be fitted with some kind of automatic alarm that would relay back to Keniclius. But there was no sign that anything of the sort existed. A moment's consideration and he realized there was no need to be concerned.

The little repair vehicle had shown a tendency to take off again. But once they'd removed its sole passenger, it stopped and now floated patiently in place.

"Agmar," began Kirk quietly, "we don't want to hurt you. You claim you're a peaceful people. Well, we're an easygoing race, too, we humans. But we must have Spock back. If this means using crude physical force against you, then rest assured we'll do so."

Agmar was not impressed. Nor was he arrogant. More than anything else his attitude smacked of resigned indifference. If he was startled to see the humans again, he didn't show it.

"I do not think that is possible," he said blandly. "The Vulcan-human blend of wisdom, sense of order, durability, reason, and strength is the finest the Master has ever found. We are pleased Spock will carry on our work."

"Patrick O'Morion!" Sulu gasped. The whole situation had been turned upside down and a new light now gleamed on its backside.

"Carry on *your* work?" was all Kirk could stutter.

"We are the last of a dying race on a dying world, Captain," intoned Agmar. A limb that remained unpinned gestured towards the ships.

"Once, we had a great mission. Then the disease destroyed nearly all of us. We five are the frail remnant of that race, the inheritors of that purpose.

"And we are sterile. We cannot put out spores. When we go, there will be no more of our kind."

"This great plan, this mission of yours," probed McCoy. "What happens to it if something happens to Spock—or to the Master?"

It was Agmar's turn to be put off-stride and confused. He recovered quickly, utilizing the response that all "masters" engender in their subjects.

"There will always be a Master. But come, you are worried about your friend, and that is needless, I assure you. I will show you that he is safe and in good condition. Better than you can guess."

He wriggled out of their relaxing grasp and shuffled into the hangar. Kirk and the others hesitated, then followed.

"Just like that, Captain?" asked Sulu. Kirk was thinking furiously, trying to stay one mental step ahead of Agmar. Yet, who could tell how the Phylosians saw things?

"Yes, just like that, Mr. Sulu. All the same, keep that bag handy." By way of emphasis he hefted his own.

"No tricks now, Agmar." The Phylosian didn't reply. He leaned forward and pressed a button on the console of the flitter.

Rapidly, the other four joined them. They dismounted from their own repair craft. Then the five moved together to stop before what looked like a solid, blank wall.

"The way is through here, gentlemen," said Agmar. He moved forward. In doing so, Kirk noticed that he stepped on a circular section of floor that was slightly different in color from the rest. Immediately, the wall slid aside to reveal a huge metallic iris behind it.

Agmar moved again and stepped on a second odd-hued round area. Now the iris dilated. An enormous tunnel appeared, a gaping wound in the earth. Its floor was smooth and sloped gently downward, under the city.

Kirk could just make out another iris far away down the tunnel. A second later it, too, opened.

Beyond was only endless blackness.

Agmar and his fellows started into the tunnel. Kirk did

not follow immediately. Nor did McCoy or Sulu. That bottomless hole looked awfully dark.

Agmar turned. "We sprang from the soil, Captain," he said reassuringly. "These tunnels are part of our ancient home." He drew a flat disk from his middle. It was somewhat larger than a voder. He did something to one side of the disk, and it suddenly put out a brilliant beam of light.

"This will serve to show our way." He turned and started down the tunnel.

Kirk wasn't keen on following, but they didn't have much choice. Beating up an already willing Agmar was a poor alternative to what appeared to be acquiesence.

"Once more into the breech," muttered McCoy.

There was more than one tunnel, they soon saw. More than two, than three. After a short walk they'd already passed dozens of intersecting corridors, a veritable labyrinth of passageways cutting through the earth beneath the city.

Sulu was busy with his tricorder.

"No wonder we couldn't detect Spock or Keniclius with shipboard scanners, Captain. Our sensor beams couldn't penetrate here."

"Absurd," McCoy objected, observing their surroundings. "It must have been interference of some kind. These walls don't look thick enough."

"Perhaps not, Doctor," admitted Sulu. "But according to tricorder analysis they're composed of artificial elements some six hundred times denser than lead, in addition to a surface force field." He shook his head wonderingly. "I can only guess at the kind of foundation they must sit on."

"On the other hand—" continued McCoy as though he'd never doubted the walls' shielding ability.

They hadn't been walking much longer before something else caught Kirk's attention. He whispered to McCoy.

"Do you hear something?"

"What, Jim?"

"I'm not sure." Kirk's brow furrowed in concentration.

"Not much further now, Captain," came Agmar's voice from just ahead.

"There it is again!" Kirk gave a sudden start and stopped, his voice rising. "A flapping sound. . . ."

That was the signal for light to leave the tunnel, and illumination of another sort to set in. They found themselves standing helplessly in blackness as black as the deepest sleep.

They'd been tricked again.

He shouted, "Use your belt lights!"

"They don't operate," replied Sulu nervously. "I've already tried."

"Agmar!" Kirk yelled angrily. "Agmar! . . ."

Agmar didn't answer.

Now McCoy and Sulu also recognized the uneven, beating sounds of the approaching swoopers. In the confined darkness of the tunnel it sounded like a growing storm. Most men are willing to face a certain amount of danger in normal circumstances.

But in the dark!

The hardest thing was to resist the urge to go charging off into nothingness, to run blindly away from the threatening noise. They might crash into a wall or, worse, there might be vertical shafts in the underground maze as well as horizontal.

They hadn't seen any pits on the way in, however. At worst it would be a quick death, a clean death. With Kirk, to think was to act.

"Run! We've got to find some light. We can't do anything unless we can see what we're fighting. Keep your hands out and feel for the walls. And keep talking—stay together!" Kirk moved away, starting in the direction he thought they'd been going.

"This way!" Then he broke into a run. McCoy and Sulu were close by. They didn't have to keep talking to stay aware of each other's position—footsteps and increasingly heavy breathing solved that.

The same sounds might also reveal their location to any pursuers, but Kirk suspected that whatever was chasing them could find them easily enough in the dark anyway.

"Don't stop!" His voice echoed like thunder down the tunnel. "DON'T STOP . . . Don't Stop . . . don't stop. . . ."

All of a sudden it sounded like they were leaving the alien cacophony further behind.

"We're gaining on them," he panted.

"Jim, up ahead!" Kirk squinted at McCoy's shout. Sure enough, there did seem to be a pinpoint of light off in the distance.

"I see it . . . I see it . . . keep going!" There couldn't be light where there was no light—that was one kind of mirage man hadn't encountered yet.

Sulu had slipped slightly behind. Unconsciously, they'd changed into the most practical order for running—McCoy barely in the lead, with Kirk in the middle and Sulu, the youngest and freshest runner, bringing up the rear.

The change from the blackness of the tunnel to the light of the room was overpowering. It was like waking up in the glare of a flashlight. They were momentarily blinded and stumbled to a halt.

The underground chamber they'd emerged into was roughly circular in shape and the by-now expected four times human size. Two other entrances gaped in the walls, leading off to unknown regions. Controls and flashing panels lined the walls.

A long table sat in the center of the room, surrounded by an attached series of fragile-looking, semitransparent crystalline globes. These formed a sparkling corona for the platform. All were connected to each other and to the delicate instrumentation built into the table.

On the table lay Mr. Spock.

McCoy hesitated just long enough to unhitch his medical tricorder before sprinting forward. Kirk and Sulu followed.

McCoy took a hurried preliminary reading from the motionless form. He checked the results, reset frantically and made another, slower pass. His eyes were wild when he finally looked over at Kirk and Sulu.

"Something's affecting his brain. All other bodily functions are normal, but he's dying."

"IT IS TOO LATE, CAPTAIN KIRK!"

They whirled as that rolling voice exploded off surrounding walls. Keniclius 5 towered over them, staring down at the tiny intruders from one of the other entrances.

"IN A LITTLE WHILE YOUR FRIEND WILL BE GONE . . . IN A WAY. BUT AS KENICLIUS 1 LIVES ON IN EACH OF HIS CLONES, SO WILL MR. SPOCK. BEHOLD, GENTLEMEN, THE DAWNING OF A NEW ERA . . . THE SALVATION OF A GALAXY . . . SPOCK 2!"

He made a grandiose gesture toward the third portal. Again Kirk, McCoy, and Sulu turned.

Another huge figure had appeared there. It had a familiar detached look, sharply peaked ears, oddly arched eyebrows. It was Mr. Spock, four times over.

His expression was not unfriendly. But neither did the giant show signs of recognition at the appearance of his shipmates, nothing to give the three officers a surge of hope.

They had only the single moment to register shock before the sounds of their tunnel pursuers grew suddenly very loud.

"Get ready!" Kirk ordered.

Now the contents of the mysterious leather sacks were revealed as the three men drew out filtering masks and slipped them over their heads. Kirk tugged the protective bag off his own device.

It was a slim cylinder with one slightly flared end. Several small nozzles protruded from that end, while the opposite sported a handhold and control knob. McCoy began fitting the fourth mask over the supine face of Spock 1.

"WEAPONS DEACTIVATORS ARE IN OPERATION HERE, TOO, CAPTAIN KIRK. A LAST CHANCE—RETURN TO YOUR SHIP."

That's when the tunnel exploded in a landscaper's nightmare. There were swoopers, too, scattered among a crawling, hopping, rolling collage of leafy, screaming monstrosities, offshoots of a plant kingdom gone mad.

Kirk, Sulu, and McCoy depressed the single control set in the base of their cylinders. Suddenly the room was enveloped in a thick chemical mist.

At first the gray fog hugged the floor. As it began to rise a strange expression came over the face of Keniclius 5. He started to cough roughly and retreated from the rapidly dimming room. No one noticed as Spock 2 did likewise.

Not only could Sulu not see Captain Kirk or Dr. McCoy in the drifting miasma, he couldn't see the cellulose abominations that were attacking them, either. But he could sure hear them. At which point the steady hiss that had been issuing from his cylindrical sprayer fizzled out.

He yelled into the mist. "The sprayer's empty, Captain!"

"Mine too, Jim!" came the familiar voice of McCoy. Sulu moved toward it, clinging tightly to the empty sprayer. They might be reduced to fighting with clubs after all.

He bumped into something solid and almost screamed. It was only McCoy.

"Wait a minute," came another voice, Kirk's. "Listen."

No one said a word. Sure enough, the plant noises had stopped. Not died out slowly, or faded, just ... stopped. McCoy tried to make out shapes in the thick haze surrounding them.

"Maybe they're waiting for this to clear. This far underground, there has to be some kind of automatic air-circulation system to blow out accumulating impurities."

Sure enough the mist started to clear, thinning even as he spoke. Soon Kirk could see the two of them. They moved to stand back to back in expectation of a renewed attack. Kirk removed his mask and sniffed.

"It's okay now."

McCoy and Sulu removed theirs. The cleaning process accelerated and the mist broke up rapidly. In seconds it was completely gone.

So were most of the plants.

Those that remained behind weren't going to attack anyone ever again. They lay on the floor, limbs twisted grotesquely, shriveled like dead clumps of hedge.

"Well, how about that," McCoy mused, studying the copse-laden battlefield. "Great-grandpappy's weed spray still works."

"I'll witness that," said a relieved Kirk, "so long as those that got away don't come back."

"I don't think they'll be in a hurry to do so, Captain," observed Sulu.

"Even so, we've got to get Spock out of here before Keniclius returns. Scott should have the ship back in orbit now." He took out his communicator, activated it.

"There's a chance this shield is directional. We might be able to beam out, even if nobody can beam in. Kirk to *Enterprise* . . . Kirk to *Enterprise*. . . ." There was no answering beep. He paused, tried again. No luck.

"Must be these blasted walls. Kirk to *Enterprise*. . . ."

McCoy had been examining Spock ever since it appeared they were safe from counterattack. Now he looked up and shook his head slowly, sadly.

"It's no use, Jim. He's fading too fast. He'll be dead inside a quarter hour." He hesitated. "He no longer thinks. His mind is gone. But it's not the normal blankness of predeath. This machine," and he indicated the instrument-laden table, "seems to be draining him somehow."

"MORE THAN JUST DRAIN, GENTLEMEN." They turned.

Keniclius was no plant. He'd returned.

"HIS MEMORIES HAVE BEEN TRANSFERRED . . . RELOCATED INTO THE MECHANISM ITSELF AND THEN TRANSFERRED AGAIN." He moved towards them.

"I CAN DUPLICATE EXACT PHYSIOLOGICAL STRUCTURES. I CANNOT DUPLICATE THAT WHICH IS LEARNED. I CAN REPRODUCE THAT SECTION OF THE MIND WHICH HOLDS THOUGHTS, BUT I CANNOT REPRODUCE THINKING. I CAN MAKE AGAIN THE AREA THAT IS RESPONSIBLE FOR MEMORY, BUT I CANNOT CREATE MEMORIES.

"JUST AS MY PREDECESSOR TRANSFERRED HIS MEMORIES AND THOUGHTS TO ME THROUGH A SIMILAR MACHINE, SO HAVE I DONE WITH MR. SPOCK AND HIS DUPLICATE."

"You talk about your cloning as though you were creating life!" screamed a frustrated Kirk. "But you have to murder to do it!"

Unexpectedly, that appeared to affect the giant. He halted in his approach, something within him seemingly in conflict with itself. Kirk noticed the hesitation. While it seemed incredible that this monster might have some distorted sense of morality, he had to grab at any chance.

Together the three of them got hold of Spock's limp

form and lifted it off the table. They started carrying him toward the third entrance.

They didn't get very far.

The second colossal figure had appeared and was blocking their retreat. Nor did the giant Spock appear inclined to move out of their way.

There was no hesitation in Kirk's voice now.

"Out of my way, mister!" he yelled at the giant. "That's an order." The huge head inclined slowly to stare blank-faced at them, but the giant showed no sign of moving. McCoy had his medical scanner out and working.

"I don't think he understands, Jim. His mind is still trying to assimilate all the fresh knowledge that's been poured into it."

That first order had come automatically. But now Kirk found himself uncertain how to proceed.

How much Mr. Spock was there in the giant towering silently over them—and how much Keniclius?

XII

On board the orbiting *Enterprise* the frustration, if not the danger, was just as intense. Wishing he had the full resources of a planet-based communications station, Scott struggled to keep his voice calm as Uhura's repeated attempts to contact the landing party met with repeated nonsuccess. He had no way of knowing, of course, that Kirk, Sulu, and Dr. McCoy were no longer on the surface of Phylos, but under it.

"Keep trying, Lieutenant. We've got to make contact with the captain."

"What do you think I've been trying to do for the past fifteen minutes, sir?" She shook her head and glared. "It's no use. I've tried every ship-to-ground frequency I can think of. No response. I can't even determine if their communicators are still operational."

"Something down there ... either the communicators have been destroyed, or there's something awfully thick between us and them."

Scott had one card left.

"All right, Mr. Arex?" The navigation officer turned back to look at the chief engineer. "I want every ohm of power on this ship, except for the life-support systematization, put behind a tight-beam communications probe. We must try to break through whatever's blocking our communications!"

"That's fine for a simple contact, Mr. Scott," concurred Uhura. "But to maintain communication on such a power load could be disastrous. We risk total drain of our dilithium crystals. Could burn out every reserve on the ship."

"Don't I know it, lass." Of all the people on the *Enterprise* to recommend such a command, he reflected ironically, the last one ought to be her chief engineer.

"But we've left orbit as the captain requested and returned. I don't know what the situation is down below, but we should have heard from them by now. And I can't order any action until I know what the situation is. We must make contact."

Kirk slumped to the floor, sat with his head bent between his knees. The giant didn't respond to a reflex command. Now Kirk had time to think, and he found himself at a complete loss. The life of his first officer—and friend—was slipping away with every tick of the chronometer, and he seemed helpless to prevent it. Helpless.

However, circumstances often take a hand where individual decisions fail. There was a deep rumbling sound. The giant Spock was clearing his throat.

Kirk's head came up. His thoughts shifted from distant regions of remorse to the present. Maybe there was a chance.

McCoy was already taking another reading on the colossus.

"He's coming out of it, Jim. Becoming conscious and aware."

Kirk scrambled to his feet and took a step toward the giant. He stopped.

What should he say? What *could* he say? Was there really anything of the Spock he'd known in this ... Frankenstein? Anything beyond surface features and superficial similarities? For that matter, how much of the original idealistic doctor remained in a Keniclius five times removed from the first?

Think, man, think! Say something, anything. . . .

He heard his voice talking. "Spock, what is the logic of letting a man die for the sake of creating his duplicate? Explain it to me, sir, explain it to me!"

The giant raised an eyebrow, thinking, but did not respond.

"Power sources are channeled, Mr. Scott," Uhura informed him. "I hope you know what you're doing, sir."

"So do I, lass, so do I. Let's find out." Uhura turned back to her console. Her hand moved toward a certain little-used switch, the switch that was used only for expensive tight-beam communications. She'd used it before, but never with this kind of power behind it.

Would the components involved be able to handle the strain of routing the full power of the *Enterprise?* She fervently hoped so.

If not, there was a fair chance the console would explode in her face. . . .

"Jim, we've got to do something!" McCoy pleaded, taking another reading on the original Spock.

"I'm trying to, really!" He eyed Spock 2. The real Spock had never been impressed by physical violence. This lumbering double would be even less so. Their only chance lay in reasoned argument.

"Look," he said desperately, "Vulcans do not condone the meaningless death of any being. Spock's death *is* meaningless, if its only purpose is to create a giant duplicate of himself. It's been proven time and again that no duplicate can possibly be as efficient as an original."

"IT IS NOT JUST A DUPLICATE!" objected an angry Keniclius. " 'AS GOOD AS AN ORIGINAL', INDEED! HE WILL BE

FAR BETTER THAN THE ORIGINAL—THE BEGINNING OF A
MASTER RACE!"

Kirk's ready reply was interrupted by a startlingly loud
beep. He looked dazedly at his communicator as if it
might suddenly jump off his belt and bite him. Then he
unclipped it and fumbled with the activator. A better idea
stopped him.

He tossed the unopened communicator to Spock 2. The
giant caught it easily in one enormous palm. If the duplicate's mind was not fully operational yet, Kirk reflected,
then all was lost. No amount of argument would serve.

At least its reflexes looked sound.

"That's our ship calling, Spock. You're her first officer.
You answer her." The beep came again.

Raising his hand, the giant appeared to study the tiny
instrument. It made no move to open it and acknowledge
the now constant beeping.

"Spock's slipping, Jim," whispered McCoy tensely.
"There isn't much time left."

"I'm sure we're getting through," Uhura insisted, the
strain in her voice reflecting the one warping the communications equipment. "But they're not replying."

"Keep trying," ordered Scott. Uhura kept an eye on an
overhead indicator. "We're nearing the overload point on
the dilithium now, Mr. Scott. Our reserves . . ."

"Keep . . . trying."

Suddenly the giant's eyes seemed to clear, his expression to brighten. With the ease of one who's performed
the same task a thousand times, yet also compensating for
the increased size of his fingers, Spock 2 flipped open the
communicator.

"COMMANDER . . . COMMANDER SPOCK HERE."

A chance, at least they had a chance, Kirk thought excitedly!

Uhura's relieved tone sounded over the communicator.
"Thank heavens! Mr. Spock, tell the captain I've located
additional information on Keniclius."

"Let's hear it, Lieutenant!" Kirk shouted, hoping his

voice would carry far enough for the communicator mike
to pick up.

Apparently it did. Uhura continued.

"I had the library research all known writings by Keniclius. Most of them border on the incoherent, but two
themes stand out, especially in his last essays.

"One is his fanaticism. The other is some idea he had
about using his projected master race as a peacekeeping
force for the entire galaxy. That's why he needed a perfect
specimen for his cloning experiments."

There was more, but a glance at the overhead indicator
ruled out any further contact. Another second and the
needle would dip into the red zone. She hurried.

"Signing off, power drain threshold!" She snapped off
the signal and slammed down several switches with the
other hand. Her sigh of relief whooshed out only after the
needle had dropped out of the yellow and back into the
green section of the gauge. Then she grinned up at Scott.

"That is what I call close, Mr. Scott."

"At least we know they're alive, and apparently okay,"
agreed Scott, in blissful ignorance. "Let's hope it was information they could use."

"Information, yeah," mused Uhura. One arm was still
trembling. She leaned on it to hide the quiver. "Did I ever
tell you the one about the one-legged jockey, Mr. Scott—?"

"Peacekeeping," echoed Kirk bitterly. "Peacekeeping!"
He shook his head and faced Keniclius. "All this has been
a waste, *Doctor* Keniclius. There's no need for any peacekeeping master race. There's been peace in the Federation now for well over fifty years."

"THAT'S A LIE!" the giant shouted, his voice washing
over them. "WHAT ABOUT THE EUGENICS WARS? THE
GALACTIC WARS? WHAT OF THE DEPREDATIONS OF THE
ROMULANS, THE KLINGONS, AND OTHERS? NOT TO MENTION
THE ENDLESS, OH, THE ENDLESS SQUABBLES AMONG THE
SO-CALLED 'ALLIED' RACES OF THE FEDERATION ITSELF?

"AN ORGANIZATION OF SPOCK DUPLICATES IS NECESSARY
TO FORCE THEM TO LIVE IN HARMONY—FOR THEIR OWN
GOOD."

Sulu muttered, "Peace through coercion. Humanity has

finally grown out of that immature philosophy, Keniclius."

"You're the fifth Keniclius," reminded Kirk. "What makes you so sure the things you see as truth aren't just old news bulletins hundreds of years out of date? Your predecessors have probably been out of touch with mankind's sociological advances for at least that long."

"That is not possible. The Master always speaks the truth," came a new voice. A new, old voice.

They turned to face the first entrance, the tunnel of horrors they'd escaped from so recently.

Agmar and his four aides stood there, watching.

"I can't understand why you've come to think of Keniclius as a 'master,'" began McCoy. "Sure, he saved you from dying—all five of you. But why should you agree with his plan for a superrace? Of what possible interest could a race of giant Spocks have for you?"

"Our fleet of ships, which you saw," Agmar replied, "was to be launched for the same purpose the Master intends. You see, there existed between our people and him a fortuitous coincidence of purpose. Disease struck us before we could carry out our own plan to impose peace on a galaxy that knew none."

"We already have peace in our Federation," snapped Kirk, "and it wasn't imposed—it was achieved from within. A real peace!" He paused.

"You have no need of Spock now. Reverse the effects of that machine and let us take him back with us."

"NO!" thundered Keniclius wildly. "THE MOLD MUST BE BROKEN." The giant's voice wavered considerably; Kirk's revelations had thrust uncertainty into two hundred fifty years of single-mindedness that had known only absolute confidence.

But it wasn't enough. The giant couldn't reverse in a moment the accumulated efforts of those two and half centuries.

McCoy was leaning over Spock 1.

"Jim, he's almost gone." Kirk thought rapidly. McCoy could do nothing. And Keniclius wouldn't. And he—he felt utterly impotent.

In fact, there was only one other being present who

might be able to save Spock now. He turned to the other giant, who'd remained impassive throughout everything.

"If you have Spock's mind, you must know the Vulcan symbol called IDIC."

"INFINITE DIVERSITY IN INFINITE COMBINATION," the great form recited.

"Comprising the elements that make up truth and beauty," finished Kirk. "Tell me, could an army of giant Spocks impose Phylosian philosophy on any other creatures, in knowing defiance of the IDIC concept?"

There was a long pause as Spock 2 considered this question. Kirk held his breath.

Finally, "I DO NOT BELIEVE SO. . . ." Kirk spun on the other giant.

"I thought so! Reverse the machine, Keniclius!"

"No!" yelled Agmar. It was the first violent exclamation the Phylosian had made. "Our dream must not be allowed to die!" He suddenly rushed at Kirk. His companions followed, trying to keep the humans from putting Spock 1 back on the machine.

Sulu let out a vibrant battle cry, intercepted Agmar and flipped him neatly over a shoulder. The Phylosians were at a tremendous disadvantage in a fight with anyone who knew judo . . . they had too many limbs that could be conveniently grabbed.

But in the ensuing melee, while the three humans battled the Phylosians, Keniclius rushed the machine. The resolution of the minions had decided the confused master. He lifted a long bar of metal. It didn't really matter that none of the humans could reach him, they couldn't have stopped him anyhow.

The heavy bar smashed through one of the crystal globes encircling the table. There was a crackling electrical discharge and the giant retreated. Several other globes exploded in a shower of glass slivers and agonized internal components.

No one was hurt, but the damage was done. The lights on the sides of the machine went out—went out in the panels lining the walls. And the slight hum which had issued from inside the table faded into nothingness.

Kirk, who'd been functioning near his mental limit ever

since they'd first entered the chamber and seen the dying Spock, lost all control. Despite the difference in their sizes and without really knowing what he intended, he charged Keniclius.

"Murderer! You've killed Spock!"

He never reached the giant. A leg as big around as a small tree stepped between him and Keniclius. He was forced to stop and look up into the face of Spock 2.

"TO PERSIST IN THIS BEHAVIOR, CAPTAIN, IS TO NEGATE THE ELOQUENCE OF YOUR PREVIOUS ARGUMENT. MAY I SUGGEST A MORE CONSTRUCTIVE COURSE OF ACTION?"

He walked around Kirk who, thoroughly puzzled, watched him advance on Sulu and McCoy. The two officers eased Spock 1 to the ground and backed away slowly.

Bending, the giant Vulcan lifted Spock 1 in a single hand. Thumb and forefinger touched the smaller man's forehead. Closing his own eyes the giant began a familiar chant.

"MY MIND TO YOUR MIND . . . MY THOUGHTS TO YOUR THOUGHTS. . . ."

"Vulcan mind touch!" exclaimed Sulu in wonder. The chamber had become a tableau of wax figures. No one moved, everyone stared at the two Spocks. Even Keniclius, whose inaction showed he'd never anticipated anything like this.

Gradually the giant's voice faded. Spock 1 fluttered an eyelid. It rose. There was the sound of a throat being cleared . . . softer, this time.

The larger Vulcan lowered the smaller model to the ground, facing Kirk.

"I am pleasantly surprised at your capacity for deductive reasoning, Captain," said Spock 1. "When you are not being bellicose, there appears to be no end to your arsenal of forensic talents."

Kirk, however, heard little if any of this. He'd lost control of himself again—motivated by a somewhat different reason, this time.

"Spock! You old! . . ."

"YOU NEEDN'T WORRY, CAPTAIN KIRK, ABOUT THE THREAT OF A MASTER RACE," rumbled Spock 2. All turned to look at him. "THERE WILL BE NO GALACTIC MILITIA. NO

OTHER SPOCKS. THE THINGS THAT COMBINE TO MAKE SPOCK A CANDIDATE FOR SUCH A TASK ALSO WOULD NOT COUNTENANCE IT."

"BUT WHAT OF MY WORK?" queried the desperate Keniclius. "IF ALL THAT I'VE FOUGHT FOR IS ALREADY ACCOMPLISHED—THE TIMES THAT I LIVED TO END ARE ALREADY ENDED—WHAT IS TO BECOME OF ME? THERE APPEARS TO BE NO REASON WHY I SHOULD CONTINUE TO EXIST. . . ."

"On the contrary, Dr. Keniclius," objected Spock 1, "I see every reason why you should remain active. Stay on Phylos with my surrogate. The concerted effort of two scientists, each with his own particular abilities and talents to enhance the other's, might yet achieve a rebirth of Phylosian civilization . . . and enable them to contribute peacefully to the Federation."

"MY THOUGHTS EXACTLY, MR. SPOCK," agreed Spock 2.

"So one might assume, Mr. Spock," agreed Spock 1.

The first officer's successful recovery had pushed all primitive revenge-thoughts from Kirk's mind.

"How does that sound to you, Dr. Keniclius? To bring life is even more important than bringing peace. If a way can be found to revitalize their race, the Phylosians have much to contribute to galactic culture."

"I . . . I WOULD BE HONORED. IF I WOULD BE ALLOWED . . . YES, YOU ARE RIGHT, CAPTAIN KIRK. THE METHODS OF THE FEDERATION HAVE INDEED CHANGED FROM WHAT I AND MY BROTHERS KNEW. . . ."

"Truly, such a thing had not been thought of." Agmar looked excited and interested now. "Such a sudden change in thinking . . . it will be difficult. . . ."

"You'll manage," said Kirk, too diplomatic to point out that they had no choice. He'd meant what he said. The Phylosians had some sterling qualities—once this master race business had been drummed out of them. He addressed the waiting Keniclius again.

"I'll report your *new* work here to the Federation Science center. Not only do I think they'll understand, they'll probably want to send out several crews to assist you."

And to make sure you don't get the urge to make any more giant clones of anything, he added silently.

Keniclius solemnly shook hands with each of them in turn. Then Agmar and his companions escorted Kirk, McCoy, Sulu, and Spock back to the surface.

When the men of the *Enterprise* left, the two giant scientists were already discussing plans for curing the Phylosians' sterility and expanding their knowledge of Phylosian culture.

Beaming up was uneventful, and there were the expected stolid greetings from Uhura, Kyle, Arex, and the rest of the officers—everyone carefully concealing his or her true emotions.

They entered the bridge where Scott—relieved, as usual—formally returned command to Kirk.

"Where to, Captain?" asked Sulu, back in his comfortable seat at the navigation console.

"Set a general course for the Omicron region, Mr. Sulu. I think everyone deserves an extended R & R, this time. I know I do!"

"Yes, *sir*!" Sulu responded gleefully.

"It's a good thing we were able to stop Keniclius," intoned McCoy, blatantly emphasizing the "we." "Imagine . . . a whole shipload . . . maybe a whole city . . . full of giant Spocks!"

He put on an expression of exaggerated horror while Spock looked over distastefully from his position at the library control and tried to ignore McCoy.

"What a terrifying thought! . . ." the good doctor continued, unstoppable. "Giant Spocks running all over the place! Spocks towering over helpless villages, running amuck through peaceful farmland . . . turning! . . ."

"It might be easier to stand than you, Doctor," interrupted Sulu inscrutably.

"What?" McCoy responded with outraged innocence. "I'm no giant."

Kirk thought he saw an unholy gleam in Sulu's eye.

"No," the helmsman admitted, "the trouble is you never stop cloning around."

McCoy chased him all the way back to engineering.

ABOUT THE AUTHOR

Alan Dean Foster was born in New York City in 1946; he currently resides in Los Angeles, where he teaches "Cinema" at Los Angeles City College. Upon graduating from UCLA in 1969 with a B.A. in Political Science and an M.F.A. in Cinema, he briefly worked in public relations. About that time, Foster began selling short stories to such magazines as *Analog, Galaxy, If, Adam,* and *Alfred Hitchcock.* His first science-fiction novel, *The Tar-Aiym Krang,* was published by Ballantine in 1972. He quickly followed that success with *Bloodhype* and, most recently, *Icerigger*—all three novels set against the same fantastic background. Foster has also adapted the jungle movie *Luana* into a popular novel for Ballantine. He is now hard at work on *Star Trek Log Nine,* continuing the adventures of the U.S.S. *Enterprise* and its crew.

STAR TREK

These are the voyages of the starship Enterprise...

Captain's log, stardate 1980.6:

Exciting adventures from television's most popular science fiction series, starring the legendary Captain Kirk, Mr. Spock, Dr. McCoy and the crew of the Enterprise—and of course, Klingons, Romulans, and Tribbles!

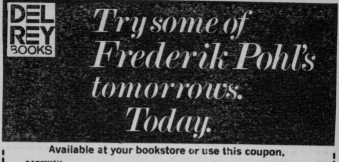

Exciting Space Adventure from DEL REY